Melissa ...

"I'll take car... little fours o...

She held his ... his deep-set eyes. She would not be intimidated by an emplo... backin...

"Okay. I'll be in the back," she sa... with a forced smile, knowing she would have to talk to him later about the boss/employee relationship. If he was going to work here, they needed to keep a few things straight.

Their eyes held a moment and she couldn't look away.

She couldn't figure out why his attitude bothered her. Brian Montclair was not her type and the last person she would want to have anything to do with beyond the bakery.

Books by Carolyne Aarsen

Love Inspired

CAROLYNE AARSEN

and her husband, Richard, live on a small ranch in northern Alberta, where they have raised four children and numerous foster children, and are still raising cattle. Carolyne crafts her stories in an office with a large west-facing window through which she can watch the changing seasons while struggling to make her words obey.

The Bachelor Baker

Carolyne Aarsen

PBR
Aar
$7.00
12/13

LC

Special thanks and acknowledgment to Carolyne Aarsen for her contribution to The Heart of Main Street continuity.

Recycling programs
for this product may
not exist in your area.

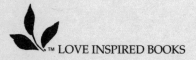

™ LOVE INSPIRED BOOKS

ISBN-13: 978-0-373-81708-5

THE BACHELOR BAKER

www.LoveInspiredBooks.com

Printed in U.S.A.

Then Jesus declared, "I am the bread of life. Whoever comes to me will never go hungry, and whoever believes in me will never be thirsty."
—*John* 6:35

I'd like to thank Dennis Donker and Candice of Barrhead Bakery for their help showing me how their bakery works. And for making me want to come back and buy every kind of pound cake they make.

Chapter One

He took up her whole office.

At least that's how it felt to Melissa Sweeney.

Brian Montclair sat in the wooden chair across the desk from her, his arms folded over his chest and his entire demeanor screaming "get me out of here."

Tall with broad shoulders and arms filling out his button-down canvas shirt rolled up at the sleeves and tucked into worn blue jeans, he looked more like a linebacker than a potential baker's assistant.

Which is what he might become if he took the job Melissa had to offer him.

Melissa drew in a deep breath, brushed her long hair back from her face and held up the worn and dog-eared paper she had been given. It held a short list of candidates for the job at her bakery, Sweet Dreams Bakery. She had already hired one of the people on the list, Amanda True, but as a high school student she was only available to work part-time.

The rest of the names, once neatly typed out, had been crossed off with comments written beside them. *Unsuitable. Too old. Unable to be on their feet all day. Just had a baby. Nut allergy. Moved away.*

This last comment appeared beside two of the eight names on her list, a sad commentary on the state of the town of Bygones, which she had only recently moved to.

When Melissa had received word of a mysterious benefactor offering potential business owners incentive money to start up a business in the small town of Bygones, Kansas, she had immediately applied. All her life she had dreamed of starting up her own bakery. She had taken courses in baking, decorating and business management, all with an eye to someday living out the faint hope of owning her own business.

When she had been approved, she had quit her baking job at the hotel in St. Louis, packed up her few belongings and come here. She felt as if her life, after all the mishaps and missteps, had finally taken a good turn. A turn she had some control over.

She started up the bakery in July and for the past month she had been running it with the help of Amanda. However, in the past couple of weeks it had become apparent she needed extra help.

She had received the list of potential hires from the Bygones Save Our Streets Committee and was told to try each of them first. Brian Montclair was on the list. At the bottom, mind you, but still on the list.

"I want to thank you for coming here," she said by way of introduction.

"No problem," he said, glancing her way, then looking suddenly away as if unable to hold her gaze. "What can I do for you?"

"The reason I called you here was to offer you a job," she said, injecting a note of enthusiasm into her voice.

Melissa still didn't know what the people on the SOS Committee were thinking when they put this man on her list. He looked like he should be pulling wrenches, not handling the delicate petit fours, tarts and cupcakes she stocked in the bakery.

Brian pulled back, his frown making his heavy eyebrows sink lower, hooding his eyes. "A job? Here? In a bakery? That's why you phoned me?"

In spite of her own concerns about his suitability, the veiled contempt in his voice raised her hackles. "Yes. I was given a list of potential hires and your name was one of the candidates."

"Seriously? The committee gave you my name?" He slapped one large hand on his blue-jeaned thigh.

She frowned herself at his shocked anger. "I was told everyone on this list was looking for work. Why else would you think I would have called you?"

"I don't know. That's why I came. To find out what you wanted. As for your list, I sure never put my name down for working in a bakery," he said, his voice full of frustration as he shoved his hand through his shaggy blond hair, his blue eyes growing hard. "The new hardware store, sure. Maybe even the bookstore that just started up, but this bakery? Seriously?"

Melissa drew in a slow breath, trying to stifle her own growing anger with his incredulity. Though she had only been running the bakery for a month now, she was proud of what she had done here.

Bygones, Kansas, she understood, had been dealt some hard economic blows the past few years. The closure of Randall Manufacturing, a major employer, had reverberated through the town, resulting in people moving away, businesses losing revenue and some even closing down.

Then, in May, someone with deep pockets set up the Save Our Streets Committee to oversee the selection of candidates to run new businesses in Bygones. Melissa had been one of the lucky applicants.

"It's a good job," she said now, a defensive note entering her voice.

"If you like working with frilly cakes and sugar and all that stuff you've got in those cases out there," Brian said, sweeping one large hand in a dismissive gesture behind him.

"I happen to enjoy it a lot."

"Well, I'm a guy. I can't see myself baking and icing cakes."

Melissa wanted to stop the interview immediately, but she knew she would have to report back to the committee and they were quite adamant about her trying to hire the people from their list.

And given that Brian was the last one on the list…

"The hours are from nine o'clock to five-thirty with half an hour off for lunch," Melissa said, forcing herself to carry on in the face of his obvious antagonism.

Brian drew in a long, slow breath, tucking his chin against his chest and looking away from her, his hair falling across his forehead. Then he looked up at her, his blue eyes like lasers. "I can't do it."

Melissa blinked, then felt the tension gripping her ease off. Brian had been the last person, in many ways, she wanted to hire.

She could still hear her friend Lily, who ran the flower shop beside her, Love in Bloom, specifically warning her not to hire the very man sitting across from her. Apparently he had been angrily vocal in his dislike of the new businesses starting up in Bygones and especially vocal about her bakery with its useless cakes and tarts.

But at the same time she knew that when she went back to the committee for a new list, she would have to show that she did all she could. So she gave it one more college try.

"I think...I think you could like working here," she said with forced enthusiasm, stifling her own frustration with his obvious reluctance. "Besides, I know there aren't many jobs available in town."

His eyes narrowed and as he leaned forward, she could almost feel the hostility radiating off him. "I don't need you to tell me that." He spoke quietly but forcefully.

"Of course," she said again, wishing she didn't feel so intimidated by him.

Brian's eyes ticked around the office with its

bare walls, then behind him, as if assessing the situation. The office was just off the sales counter of the bakery. Through the door she saw a portion of the glass cases holding the squares, cupcakes, tarts, cookies and pies she had baked this morning. Her feet still throbbed from being on them since five o'clock this morning, but it was a good feeling.

Brian turned back to her and pressed his hands against his thighs as he stood, filling up the small space even more.

He drew in a deep breath, his lips pressed together, and gave her a curt nod. "Thanks for the job offer, but no thanks."

He held her gaze a split second more and for the tiniest moment, Melissa felt a nudge of regret. In another time and another place she could acknowledge his rugged good looks, the line of his jaw.

But not here. And not now.

And not after what Jason did to you.

Melissa buried that thought again. Jason was in the past. She was in another time and a better place and she was her own person and her own boss in charge of her own life.

Girl's got to take care of herself because no one else will.

Her mother's constant mantra rang through her mind as she got to her feet.

"Thanks for coming in," she said, trying not to let her relief show.

Brian held her gaze another moment, as if he could sense her relief, then he gave her another curt nod, turned and marched out of her office, around the counter and out the door.

When she heard the door fall shut behind him, she dropped back in her chair. Her hands were still shaking. Goodness he was upset and she shouldn't be surprised.

At least this obligation had been taken care of. She could strike his name off her list.

The next thing to do was call Dale Eversleigh, her contact person on the SOS Committee, and let him know she had done her best with the names the committee had given her. Surely there had to be someone else in Bygones who was not only capable but willing to work in her bakery.

Just then the buzzer sounded, announcing another customer. Melissa glanced at the clock on the wall of her office. Amanda was still busy in the back. So Melissa caught the pink-and-white-striped apron off a hook, slipped it on and went out to greet her next customer.

A young man stood in the center of the bakery, hands in his pockets, brown hair brushed back from a narrow face frowning as a young woman flitted along the glass cases oohing and aahing over the contents, her dark ponytail bobbing as she crouched down and then straightened as she inspected everything. The cases held cupcakes with pink fluffy icing, cookies spread out on white paper doilies, cakes with pink trim and trays and trays of sugary squares and puffs piled up in fancy little displays. "Would you look at all the good stuff here?" she said, her voice full of awe.

"I'm looking at the prices," the young man said, frowning at the blackboard Melissa had up on one wall with the amounts written on it. Amanda, the young girl who worked at the bakery, had written the list of offerings up in colored chalk, decorating it with fanciful flowers and flourishes. "Now that Dad's not working anymore I can't afford anything here."

"But, Rory, it's all so lovely," the young girl said, pouting at him as she rested her hand against the case as if trying to touch the tarts inside. "I'm sure it's worth every penny."

"And I don't have as many pennies since Dad got laid off from the police department," Rory said. "We can grab a chocolate bar at The Everything around the corner. Be way cheaper."

"But not as good." In spite of her reluctance, however, the young girl straightened and with one last, longing look at the pastries gave Melissa an apologetic smile. "Sorry."

Then they left.

Another satisfied customer. Though the bakery was busy enough to require extra help, she had come across resistance to her prices—even though they were more than fair—and resistance to her presence. Small towns, she thought, turning away from the counter, Brian's unwilling countenance slipping into her thoughts.

"Sorry I wasn't helping you," Amanda called as she came out of the storage room at the back of the bakery lugging a large yellow pail. Tall and thin, with curly brown hair and what Amanda said were True Blue eyes, she didn't look strong enough to carry the large bags of flour and pails of shortening Melissa used. "I saw you were busy with Mr. Montclair so I figured I'd get the shortening out to soften. But I couldn't find it right away and had to go digging." She set the pail down on the wooden counter, her hair coated with a layer of dust. "What's the matter? You look ticked."

"It shows?" Melissa pushed out her lower lip and blew her bangs out of her face with a sigh of frustration. "I just lost a customer and tried to hire Brian Montclair."

"You tried to hire Brian?" Amanda looked at her, her blue eyes wide with surprise. "I heard him at The Everything when the bakery first started, you know, saying he wasn't comin' to any of the new businesses if he could help it. 'Wasn't working for no city slickers,' he said." Amanda's last words rose up as if on a question. "Surprised he would come for an interview."

Though only a teenager, Amanda was a life-long resident of Bygones and had been filling Melissa in on the many and varied people living in the town, their history and connections.

"He didn't know it was an interview when he came," she said. "But he didn't want the job."

"Not surprised. He's more of a mechanic than a baker."

Guess she had him pegged after all, Melissa thought.

"Got lotsa cake pops left," Amanda said as she pried open the lid on the pail. "We don't need to make any tomorrow."

"That's too bad. I thought they would sell better," Melissa said, picking up her checklist for what they needed to make for tomorrow. "Back in St. Louis there was a bakery around the corner from the hotel I baked at that couldn't keep up with the demand. Lots of mothers had them at birthday parties."

"They're great and all, but people need to try them, I guess. Maybe if Mrs. Morgan has them at the wedding—"

Melissa held her hand up as if to stop what Amanda had to say. "Don't even say that out loud or somehow she'll find out and she'll add them to an already overstuffed dessert menu."

Amanda grinned. "She is kinda getting carried away."

"Kinda," Melissa agreed, glancing over the amount of squares and cookies still in the case. "At least today we don't have as much left as yesterday."

She eased out another sigh, rubbing her left temple with her fingertips as she hung the clipboard back on the nail beside the industrial mixer. She'd been up since five o'clock this morning getting the bread going for the day and a spike of pain was slowly drilling into her temple.

"You look beat," Amanda said. "Why don't you go home? I'll be okay to close."

Melissa glanced around the bakery trying not to make a face at the flour dusting the floor, the crumbs spread around the cutting boards and the fingerprints she knew smudged the display cases in the front. Though she had dreamed for many years about opening her own bakery, the reality of the relentlessness of the work was settling in.

As did the fact that the success of the bakery lay squarely on her shoulders. In St. Louis, working at the hotel as a baker, she was an employee. Here, she was on her own. Though independence and the ability to support herself were what she had always wanted, she never realized how heavy the load could be.

"Okay. If you don't mind cleaning up," she said.

"Sure. No problem." Amanda flashed her a smile.

With a grateful sigh Melissa tugged her apron off just as her cell phone rang. Her heart sank as she glanced at the name displayed on the screen.

Mrs. Morgan. Mother of the groom of the wedding Melissa was baking for. Very demanding mother of the groom, she might add.

"My dear Melissa. Sorry to be a bother," Mrs. Morgan was saying in her usual hurried and breathless voice. "But I need to meet with you and Gracie. I want to rethink the dessert reception."

Of course she did, Melissa thought, leaning against the counter behind her. "When did you want to meet?"

"Tomorrow. At noon at the Cozy Cup."

"Okay. I'll be there." She ended the call and blew out her breath, catching Amanda's concerned look. "Will you be able to help me at noon tomorrow for an hour or so?"

Amanda nodded. "My mom doesn't need me then. I can easily come."

"That would be great." She pushed herself

away from the counter and walked into her office. Right now her first priority was to talk to Dale Eversleigh and see about getting a new list of prospective employees.

Brian strode across Bronson Avenue feeling more humiliated with each step. Working at the bakery? What was the SOS Committee thinking?

When Melissa Sweeney had called him he wasn't sure what she wanted, but she had asked him to come to the bakery and it would seem weird to say no. The first time he'd seen her around town he had been immediately attracted to the spunky redhead with the bright smile.

That was until he found out that she was the owner of the new bakery. A business that had received the money he also had applied for.

He yanked his keys out of his pocket, still frustrated that the SOS Committee had seen fit to give money to outsiders for shops like a pet store, flower shop, bookstore, coffee shop and bakery instead of the mechanic shop he'd wanted to open. The hardware store he could understand, but the rest?

And now the committee seriously thought he would want to work at the bakery? The hardware store, okay, but the bakery? Seriously?

He was about to cross Main Street to where

his truck was parked by the grocery store when the door of the Cozy Cup Café opened and Miss Coraline stepped out.

"Brian. Hello," she said, giving him the same warm smile she seemed to have for all her former students.

Miss Coraline was tall, always elegant, her silvery hair cut the same she had always worn it, a short style brushing her jaw. As far as Brian could tell she hadn't aged since she taught him in high school.

"Hello, Miss Coraline," he said, spinning his truck keys around his finger, stifling the frustration still simmering below the surface of his own smile.

"I noticed you just came out of the bakery," she said, a surprised note in her voice. Brian suspected she remembered his rant about the new businesses at the Grand Opening.

"Yeah. I...uh...got a call from Miss Sweeney. Said she wanted to talk to me about something." He stopped himself there. If anything, he was even more angry than he had been then. Bad enough that the SOS Committee turned down his request, but now they wanted him to work for one of the people who had been chosen instead of him?

Miss Coraline raised an eyebrow. "Something

seems to be bothering you. Do you want to talk about it?"

Brian seethed a few more seconds, gave his truck keys another spin then blurted out, "Why did you and the SOS Committee seriously think I would want to work at the bakery?"

Miss Coraline looked taken aback at his anger. Then she held out a placating hand. "I thought it would work for you. After all, you did take my Home Economics class. You seemed to enjoy the baking."

That was mostly because Lexi was in it and he'd been eyeing her for a couple of months. But he wasn't telling Miss Coraline that. "I didn't exactly pass."

Miss Coraline gave him a gentle smile. "I understand, but some of the other people needing work seemed more suited to the other businesses. I didn't have the final say who got on what list, if that's any consolation," Miss Coraline said. "But if you don't want to work at the bakery, you don't have to."

"I suppose not," Brian muttered.

"However, you might as well know the other businesses all have their own list of people to ask and if you don't take this job, you probably won't get one with the other stores."

Not that he wanted to work at a pet store or

flower shop either, but it seemed his options were growing narrower and narrower.

"I just need something until business picks up," Brian said. "I've got a few mechanic jobs coming in…" He let the sentence drift off, not so sure he wanted Miss Coraline to know exactly where things lay for him. He'd heard rumors that Mr. Robert Randall was looking for financing. Maybe he was opening the factory again in spite of what Randall had said when he laid them off. But for now, he needed work.

"You'll have to make your own decision. Pray about it and see what happens," she said.

Brian released a light laugh. He'd spent a lot of time with God the past half year. Ever since he got his pink slip from Mr. Randall. Ever since he watched the town he loved slowly die off.

"I'll do that," he said, glancing at his watch. "I'm sorry, but I gotta run. I'm picking up my grandfather from Concordia. He's coming for a visit."

"You say hello to him from me, and I hope to see him around while he's here."

"You probably will. He's been talking about moving back here."

"Wouldn't that be lovely?" Miss Coraline said.

"Yeah. Real nice." The only problem was his grandfather would need a place to stay and that would likely be the house Brian had inherited when his parents died. But Brian was still making payments on it and if Grandpa moved in with him, Brian would need more than the sporadic mechanic work he had been getting to support the two of them.

You might have to take that job at the bakery after all.

He gave Miss Coraline a tight smile. "I better get going. I'll see you around," he said, then strode across the street to his truck.

As he drove out of town, he heaved a sigh, his mind spinning in circles, thinking about Melissa Sweeney, her job offer and his own situation.

When Randall Manufacturing closed its doors, he was out of a job. He'd worked as a foreman and had made decent money. Enough that he'd managed to set some aside with the hope of starting his own mechanic shop. He had been working on cars and trucks ever since he could pick up a wrench, helping his father work on farm equipment and fixing up his and his sister's vehicles. He'd been doing some work on the side with an eye to someday owning his own business. Being his own boss.

After he lost his job he thought that would be the push he needed to get it started. So he'd gone to the bank for a loan. But the bank had turned him down, stating that his down payment wasn't large enough given the current economic condition of the town.

His hopes had been revived when he'd heard about some mystery person with a large amount of money who was looking to start new businesses in Bygones. That hope had been extinguished in favor of outsiders. The committee was looking for new blood. New ideas.

Why had a local like him, who had way more invested in Bygones, been turned down in favor of someone who wasn't from here, who couldn't possibly care about the town the way he did?

Bunch of city slickers like Melissa Sweeney. He gripped the steering wheel of his truck, stifling his humiliation. In spite of his antagonism to Melissa as City Slicker Baker, he couldn't stop noticing Melissa was an appealing woman. She was the first girl he had felt any kind of attraction toward in a while. In another time and in other circumstances he might allow that feeling to go somewhere. But not now.

He had no job and no prospects.

Nothing to offer her.

Chapter Two

"I may as well warn you—Trent's mother wants to meet with us to talk about another change to the dessert menu." Gracie Wilson ran her fingers through her short brown hair, artfully disheveling her cute pixie cut as she blew out a sigh. "And she was talking about adding a tea right after the church service. Said it was a courtesy for the people who attended the service who we didn't invite to the reception."

Melissa caught a curious note in Gracie's voice. "Is everything okay?" she asked. "You seem upset."

Gracie waved off Melissa's concerns. "I feel overwhelmed by all this fuss and bother. Mrs. Morgan is all about pink and girlie and I want things simple. I can't believe how much planning she's been doing. Plus, I wish we would have kept the wedding on a Saturday, the way

I originally wanted. I just think she wants as many people there as possible."

"A Sunday wedding will be very nice," Melissa said, putting her hand on the young girl's arm in a gesture of commiseration. "And if it's any consolation my mother had been planning my wedding for years. In fact, before she died, she gave me a folder with ideas she collected."

"I didn't know your mother was dead," Gracie said, her voice full of consternation. "That's so sad."

Melissa waved off her concern. "It happened five years ago."

Gracie was quiet, then she leaned forward. "Have you met anyone since you came here who would give you a reason to pull that folder out?"

"I've met lots of people," Melissa said, being deliberately obtuse.

"You know what I mean." Gracie leaned closer, grinning, her previous funk disappearing behind her usual bubbly personality. "What do you think of my boss? Patrick Fogarty? Isn't he just a dream?"

"He is good-looking."

"That sounds like a brush-off. So, have you met someone else then?"

Just then the door opened. When Melissa looked up she had a sense of déjà vu.

Brian Montclair stepped into the Cozy Cup

Café followed by an elderly man, tall, slender, wearing a golf shirt and plaid shorts. His hair, a thick shock of white, was neatly brushed and his blue eyes sparkled. He had the same widow's peak as Brian, the same blue eyes. Melissa guessed this was Brian's grandfather.

Brian glanced her way, then he hesitated a moment and she wondered if he would come up to her and accept her offer. Instead he turned to the man he was with.

"Grandpa, what did you want to drink?" Brian asked him.

Gracie glanced over her shoulder, then turned back to Melissa, grabbing at her arm, her eyes wide. "Oh. My. Goodness. He *likes* you," she said in a stage whisper.

Melissa shot her a frown. "What? Who?"

"Brian. He totally likes you."

Melissa resisted the urge to roll her eyes but lowered her voice, too. "That man has been nothing but cranky to me, especially when…" She stopped herself there, figuring someone like Brian wouldn't want Gracie to know about her offering him a job.

But Gracie didn't catch her vague sentence; instead, she looked back just as Brian glanced their way. Then she turned back to Melissa, her eyes wide with pleasure. "See? He is checking you out."

"He's wondering what you're whispering about."

"He's acting like my brothers do when they like someone."

As a sister of five brothers, Gracie could be considered an expert on male behavior. Melissa, growing up the only child of a single mother, had no such experience on which to base her judgment.

However, she figured she knew how a man would act if he was attracted to someone. The first thing Jason had done when he met her was flirt with her. Then give her his phone number. When they dated, he made her believe she was the only one for him. That he would always be there for her. They talked about starting up a new business together—a bakery in St. Louis. She moved to be with him and make their plans. But just when everything seemed to come together, he left her with her money, her dreams and a broken and disillusioned heart.

Melissa pushed the dark memory aside. She had her bakery now and her own chance to prove herself. Depending on anyone to fulfill her or to support her plans was a waste of time and emotion.

Brian reminded her too much of Jason. A bit arrogant and a bit controlling. No thanks. She was her own boss now, in charge of her business and her heart, and she wasn't letting anyone in on either one.

Then the door of the shop opened again and Mrs. Morgan swept in.

"Oh, dear," she heard Gracie whisper as Mrs. Morgan walked toward them, clutching a binder identical to the one Gracie had on the table in front of her.

"Good afternoon," Mrs. Morgan said. "Sorry I'm late."

She held out her hand to Melissa, her red fingernails flashing. Her hair, a delicately washed silver, hung in a stylish pageboy around a face that defied her actual age. Her silky brown dress seemed unnecessarily formal for a casual meeting in a coffee shop, but Melissa was slowly learning Mrs. Morgan placed much stock in appearances. She didn't so much sit down as ease into the chair in one fluid motion. "What have I missed?" she asked, glancing from Melissa to Gracie.

"We were talking about some of the changes you wanted to make." Gracie's voice grew small in this woman's presence.

"Gracie said you wanted to add a tea with snacks for after the service," Melissa said, taking over, hoping to ease the sudden tension. "However, this will substantially change the cost."

Gracie spoke up. "I don't know if my father wants—"

"You don't have to worry about the money," Mrs. Morgan said. "I told your father we would cover everything."

"But—"

"Please. I don't want to hear about it any-more." Mrs. Morgan smiled, but the tension around the table had increased.

And when the café's door burst open, Melissa jumped.

"Melissa," a worried voice called out. "I need you to come to the bakery."

Melissa turned to see Amanda scurrying toward her, twisting her apron around her hands, her face a grimace of concern. "The oven quit working and all those cupcakes you put in aren't baking."

"Did you call Alan?" Melissa asked, her mind scrambling. "He was the one who installed the stove and oven."

"He can't come until tomorrow," Amanda said. "He's working in another county today. What are we going to do?"

Melissa bit her lip, her mind racing. The cup-cakes were for a conference in Junction City.

If the organizers there liked what she had to offer, it could increase business for the bakery and maybe raise the profile of Bygones and the new businesses here.

And Mrs. Morgan was still waiting.

"So the oven won't go on at all?" Melissa asked, taking care of her first priority.

Amanda shook her head, her brown ponytail bobbing.

"I'll tell Brian. He's really handy. I'm sure he can help," Gracie said, then, before Melissa could protest, jumped to her feet as if relieved to have a reason to escape. She hurried over to where Brian sat with the older man and murmured something to him. Melissa looked away when she saw him frown, but then Brian strode over.

"Something wrong with your oven?" he asked.

"It doesn't work," Amanda said before Melissa could protest that everything was fine, which it wasn't. She didn't want Brian in her bakery. Especially not after the way he seemed to treat it so dismissively. "Could you come and fix it?" Amanda asked.

"Sure. I'll have a look at it."

"It's fine. We can manage," Melissa said, holding up her hand as if to stop him.

Brian shot her a frown. "How? Amanda said

Alan can't come till tomorrow. Can't bake your fancy cakes if your oven doesn't work."

Melissa stifled another protest at his blunt assessment of her situation. Much as she didn't like it, Brian was right.

"Okay. You can come and have a look at it," she said, relenting.

"Thanks. I think."

As Melissa held his steady gaze she caught the hint of a mocking smile teasing one corner of his mouth.

Her heart did a slow flop at the sight. Then she caught herself midreaction. Was she crazy? The man clearly didn't like her or her bakery. Why was she even the least bit attracted to him?

Because, she thought as she strode out of the coffee shop, in spite of her innate need for independence and her burning desire to make her own way in the world, there were times she wondered what it would be like to have someone beside her.

Just not this guy, Melissa reminded herself.

"So I relit the pilot light." Brian pushed himself away from the oven and, brushing the dust and crumbs off his shirt and pants, picked up his tools and got to his feet. "The oven should work now."

It hadn't taken him long at all to get Melissa's

oven going. The thermocouple wasn't working so all it took was a quick run down to the new hardware store. Thankfully, Patrick there knew his stuff and had one in stock.

Replacing it was a simple job, but it made him feel useful again. Something he didn't feel so often these days.

Melissa looked at the oven, then back at Brian as if she wasn't sure she should believe him.

"Are you sure it will work?"

"Of course I am."

"Okay." She turned the knob of the oven, listening.

Brian heard a reassuring whoosh as the gas ignited.

"Great. Wonderful," she said. "I thought I would have to start all over with the cupcakes." She turned to Amanda. "Can you get them out of the refrigerator and put them in the oven? They'll take a little longer to cook because they're cold so adjust the time by about fifteen minutes." Then she turned back to Brian with a grateful smile that didn't help his equilibrium.

Something about this woman made him feel edgy, and he didn't like feeling that way.

"Thanks again. I appreciate the help," she said, giving Brian a grateful smile. "So, what do I owe you?"

"Nothing." He'd only been here twenty minutes and half of that time was spent getting the panels off so he could get at the broken thermocouple.

"No. Really. I insist on paying you. I would have had to pay Alan and you saved my cupcakes. So how much?"

"I'm not that busy," he said with a shrug. "It's not like you dragged me away from my job."

"All the more reason to pay you," she said. "I'm sure you could use the money."

Brian felt a sliver of cold slip down his spine. Bad enough that the comment was partly true.

That she was the one to say it only added to the humiliation piling on him the past few days. He thought the final straw had been her offering him a job in the bakery, but this was worse.

He turned away from her and the only sound in the heavy silence following her comment was the hollow thunk of the lid of his metal toolbox falling shut. Then the snap of the clasps.

"I'm good" was all he said, yanking the toolbox off the floor.

"I'm so sorry," she said. "I didn't mean... It came out wrong."

His only reply was to turn and stride out of the bakery, his booted feed thudding on the floor.

He headed down the sidewalk toward his truck, dropped the toolbox in the back of his truck with a heavy clang, then glanced back, checking for his grandfather.

A couple of minutes later Grandpa came walking down the sidewalk, a frown on his face. He was probably going to give him a reaming out for walking out on a lady, Brian thought, jingling his keys.

He knew he had been rude, but her comment was ruder.

However, as Grandpa drew close, the only expression Brian saw on his features was sympathy. Which was humiliating.

They got in the truck and drove out of Bygones in silence.

When they got home Brian parked the truck in front of the house and turned to his grandfather.

"Will you be okay on your own for the next hour? I need to get some work done."

Thankfully his grandfather simply nodded and as he headed to the house, Brian went to his already tidy garage to clean up. He really didn't have any work to do, but he needed some time alone. Time to think.

He rearranged his tools on his worn workbench, then pulled out a broom, wishing for the umpteenth time he had a bigger garage to work in. A truck could barely fit inside the space. He needed room for a hoist and a lift and a much larger space for tools. He could only take on a few small jobs because of the lack of space.

Unbidden came Melissa's voice and her painful words. "…you could use the money."

He attacked the floor with the broom, sending what little dust was left flying as he struggled to dislodge the shame crawling through his belly at her words.

And the anger they created.

The ringing of his cell phone pulled him back from his frustration. He looked at the number. It was his old high school friend Kirk.

Kirk used to live in Bygones and work with Brian at the factory. When he got laid off, he and his pregnant wife, Abby, moved to Junction City. Kirk got a job driving a long-haul truck for a trucking company. He'd told Brian, if he was interested, he could get him a job there, too.

"So I called my boss and told him about you," Kirk said when Brian answered. "Told him you might be looking for a job."

Brian felt a lift of anticipation. Long-haul trucking wasn't the kind of job he wanted, but then, neither was working at a bakery, which, right now, was his only other option. "What did he say?"

"The only work he could get is relief work. You'd get a few trips a month, but if you do good with that, you might be able to work it into a full-time position."

"And how long would that take?"

"Half a year. Maybe more. Depends on how things pick up."

"I can't live off those kind of wages."

"You can't live off what you're getting now. But you could totally live with me and Abby."

Brian glanced over the yard that had been his home since he was born. Large trees shaded the house to his right. Some of them had been planted by his parents when they were still alive. Some by his grandfather, who owned the property when it was still a farm. Ahead of him lay the pasture he and his father had fenced two years before his father died.

He and his sisters had inherited the farm when his parents died. They subdivided the yard site off what was left from the farm. Brian got the house and ten acres. The girls got the money from the sale of the land. Everyone was happy. Though the girls didn't want to live in Bygones, they were thrilled their childhood home would still be available for them.

When Brian worked at the factory he often imagined the day he would drive back to the house he had grown up in to find his wife waiting for him, their children running down the driveway toward him just as he and his sisters did when their father came back from working the fields. But Brian was twenty-nine now and no closer to the family he had always dreamed of. And now he had no way of supporting this phantom family.

Even if he took this job in Junction City.

"That would mean selling my place. I can't afford to pay rent and the payments on here." The thought of selling a place that had been in his family for four generations stuck in his throat. "Let me think about this for a while," Brian continued. "I don't want to make a hasty decision."

"I know, but I'm still telling this guy about you. Send me your résumé and I'll give it to him. Maybe something else will come up in his branch in Concordia."

Brian bit his lips, then nodded. "Okay. I'll do that. Thanks for thinking of me."

"Hey, what are friends for? I'd love to work together again. Just like old times."

"Yeah. Like old times." Brian doubted anything would be like old times. Life was moving on and things were changing.

Brian said goodbye and dropped the phone in his shirt pocket, his thoughts chasing each other around his mind.

Should he take this job? Was he being foolish

hanging on to this place, clinging to the hope that Randall would start up the factory again?

Can you turn your back on your childhood home? Your father's childhood home?

He had to be realistic. Do what needed to be done. If the part-time job turned into a full-time one, then he couldn't let sentiment interfere with the reality of making a living.

Please, Lord, help me to let go of my worries. Help me to know what I should do.

"Are you busy?"

His grandfather's quiet request broke into Brian's prayers.

"No. Just thinking too much," Brian said, giving his grandfather a wry smile. He grabbed a plastic lawn chair and set it down in front of the garage. "Here. Have a seat."

His grandfather eased himself into the chair, his hands resting on his bony knees as he looked out over the yard. "Many good memories here," he said. "I miss this place."

"Do you regret moving away?" Brian asked, leaning his shoulder against the doorframe, his arms crossed over his chest, his own thoughts still spinning.

"I moved because I couldn't face the thought of living in Bygones without your parents around. It was hard enough after your grandmother passed on, but after your parents died, I wanted to leave this place behind me."

Brian's mind ticked back to that horrible time after the car accident that had killed his parents. He was still working at the plant when it happened, though his sisters had lived away from Bygones for a number of years by then.

Holly and Louisa had always said that Bygones would be a blip in their rearview mirror once they graduated. Both had held true to that promise after high school.

Brian had never understood his sisters' desire to live in the city. He needed to stay here. He craved the security he got from his job, his community of friends and his faith. He needed the quiet he could depend on receiving when he stood outside and watched the clouds chase each other across a broad expanse of Kansas sky.

He had always wanted to stay in Bygones and raise his family here. That had always been his main goal in life.

Now the promise of a job lay before him.

Part-time work, maybe, and you'd have to move in with Kirk and Abby and move away from here.

The only other option available to him right now was the bakery job. That he even considered it showed him how far things had fallen in his life and his plans.

"That was a hard time," Brian agreed, pushing his negative thoughts aside. "I understood why you wanted to leave."

His grandfather sighed. "It was hard. Especially coming so soon after your grandma died. But I think I made my decision to leave too hastily."

Brian wasn't surprised to hear the yearning in his grandfather's voice. Every time Brian visited his grandfather at the home he lived in, all his grandfather could talk about was Bygones.

"You do love it here," Brian continued. "Lots of memories."

His grandfather smiled, leaning forward in the chair as he pointed out the apple trees in the orchard. "I remember planting those with your grandmother. We planted the rootstock, and she budded them. Then she tended them and pruned them. Always were her trees. Used to make the best pies and applesauce from them."

"She loved gardening, didn't she?"

"Oh my, yes. All the shrubs and plants around this place were ones she put in." He carried on, telling Brian stories he knew by heart. With each story Brian heard the love and pining in his voice for this place that held so many memories.

He should move back here.

The thought settled into Brian's mind with a certainty he couldn't shake off. But he wouldn't say anything yet. Not until he figured out exactly how he could support them if he stayed.

He watched his grandfather walk back up to the house, pausing at the orchard and smiling. Then he carried on, reaching out to touch the shrubs lining the driveway, stopping to stoop over a blooming dahlia, looking up as crows danced and darted on the gentle wind.

He belonged here. That much Brian knew.

You could take that job in the bakery. Then he could stay.

Brian cringed at the thought, but at the same time the idea wouldn't leave him. His options were growing narrower and narrower.

He blew out a sigh, his practical mind fighting with the vision he'd had of his life. Never, in any iteration of his thoughts and dreams, had working at a bakery been part of that.

Even as he sorted things out, he sensed with each passing minute he edged closer to the decision he couldn't avoid.

Behind all of those thoughts came another chilling one. He would be working with Melissa.

Who would be his boss.

Chapter Three

Brian stood in front of the bakery early Saturday morning, hands planted on his hips as he looked at the gold swirly logo on the window. This was it. His last chance.

As he pushed open the door, his mind flashed back to the last time he was here.

"You could use the money."

Melissa's words still stung but the problem was, she was right and that was why he was here.

He swallowed his pride and stepped inside the bakery, a buzz above his head announcing his arrival.

He glanced around the inside, his eyes ticking over the wooden shelves covering the wall to his right. They were filled with loaves of freshly baked bread lined up haphazardly, as if someone was in a rush to put them out.

The glass cases to his left held cookies,

squares, cupcakes and stuff he didn't even recognize but figured he would soon.

A movement in the back of the bakery caught his attention and then, there was Melissa, wiping her hands on a towel, a welcoming smile on her face.

That faded when she saw him.

Great beginning, he thought.

"Can I help you?" she asked, her voice polite but cool.

His throat closed off as the words stuck, but he forced them out.

"I need to talk to you. About the job."

Melissa frowned, her head tipped to one side as if she wasn't sure who he really was.

"If it's still available, that is," he added.

"It is. For sure." She wiped her hands a bit more, then laid the hand towel aside. "When can you start?"

As if he had anything else going in his life.

"Now."

She hesitated. "As in right now?"

"I thought you needed help." Dread clutched at his stomach.

"I do. I do…" She caught the side of her lip between her teeth, as if thinking.

"Did someone else get the job?"

"No. Not yet. I have to talk to Mr. Eversleigh yet."

Brian wasn't sure what that was about, but he was surprised at his relief.

"I can start Monday if you prefer," he said.

"No. May as well start right now." Melissa brushed her hands over her apron and gave him a polite smile. "Come into my office and we can get some of the paperwork out of the way and get you started."

Brian fought down his hesitation.

It's only until something better comes along, he reminded himself.

Once that happened, he was out of here.

He followed Melissa into the office, feeling as if the walls were closing in on him. She sat down and pulled some papers out of a drawer.

"Fill these out. Let me know when you're done and we can go over the basics." Her words were clipped and Brian suspected she was about as willing to hire him as he was to work here.

Oh, this was going to be fantastic.

But he only nodded at her, then took the pen she handed him and started filling in the blanks.

Ten minutes later he was done. He left the papers on the desk and walked to the back of the bakery.

Melissa was dumping some flour into an industrial-sized mixer. She looked up when he came in. "Done?"

"Yeah."

"Good."

Great conversation. This was going to be just swell.

Melissa wiped her hands again, then walked past him to the front of the bakery, stopping at the front counter. "I thought you could start with taking care of customers, stocking the cases and organizing the stockroom."

"And baking?"

"I take care of that," she said, a brusque note in her voice.

"I thought you needed full-time help."

"I do, but for now you can start with this." She leveled him a narrowed gaze. "I hope that's not a problem?"

Brian held his hands up. "No problem. I just figured I'd have to be making cupcakes or some such thing."

"I like to be in charge of the baking." She said it with such a firm note in her voice, Brian pegged her immediately.

Control freak. Not that it mattered to him if he didn't do any baking. This job was strictly a fill-in.

"This is the cash register, obviously," she said, changing the subject. She pointed to a machine sitting on the wooden counter at right angles to the display cases. "People can pay cash or use their debit or credit card." Melissa demonstrated, her fingers flashing over the keys. Brian tried to keep up but figured he would find out by trial and error how the thing worked.

"I'll be in the back most of the day and when I'm not, Amanda is around. She comes at noon and stays for the afternoon. She knows how to run the cash register, too."

Melissa gestured at a chalkboard on the wall behind her. "This is a list of the prices of the goods. I also have a master list of what I've baked for the day in the back. When the stock gets low, check the list first to see how much we need compared to how much we make on average."

Melissa pointed out another checklist, rattled off some more information about stock and overages, words spilling out of her mouth faster than oil out of a busted hydraulic hose.

"Hey, Miss Sweeney," he said, holding up his hand to stem the verbal flow. "You're throwing too much at me too quick. Why don't we take this one step at a time? Let me learn as I go."

"Okay," she said, her gaze flicking away from his. "I'm usually in the back so I'm available."

"Good. Then I'll start with memorizing the price list."

Melissa nodded, then, avoiding his eyes, walked to the supply room just off the front of the bakery.

Brian blew out a sigh as he looked around the front of the bakery. Well, this was it. His new job. And from the way Melissa was acting, it was as if she wasn't too impressed with having him as an employee either.

As Miss Coraline said, God moves in mysterious ways.

"One other thing I need from you," Melissa was saying as she came out of her office carrying a bag. "You'll have to wear this."

Brian opened the bag, pulled out an apron with broad pink-and-white stripes, then stared at Melissa in dismay. "Seriously?"

"Seriously." Melissa gave him another pinched-lip look and he stifled yet another flicker of humiliation.

"Looks too small," he said, grimacing as he held it up.

"I had ordered a couple extra because I had assumed if I hired someone I would be hiring…" She paused, shrugged.

"Another woman," he finished for her. He blew out a sigh and slipped the top loop of the apron over his head. The bottom of the apron, instead of coming to his knees like hers did, hit him midthigh. Well, his indignity was complete. God was definitely trying to teach him humility.

It's for Grandpa.

"I can order another one."

"No. I'm good." As he knotted the ties at the back he couldn't help think of the phrase "tied to a woman's apron strings." That was him. "So, what do you want me to start with?"

"You could start with them," Melissa said as the door of the bakery opened and two men came inside. "I'll be in the back if you need me."

He held her gaze for a heartbeat, then turned to his first customers of the day. His heart sunk as Don Mankowski and his ever-present friend, Jake Fry, stood in front of him.

Don was almost as tall as Brian but heavier. He wore tight T-shirts in all weather to show off the muscles he worked diligently to maintain. His short cropped black hair made him look tougher than he really was, but Don was all about presentation.

Jake was shorter than Don, not as heavily built, blonde where Don was dark and not as full of swagger and self-importance. A decent guy but too attached to his sneering buddy.

Jake and Don had played football with Brian in high school and had also worked at the factory, albeit under him.

Don elbowed Jake as he tilted his rounded chin toward Brian. "Well, look who's serving up pastries. Our old boss, Mr. Montclair."

Jake gave Brian a lopsided grin. "Hey, Brian. Didn't expect to see you here."

Didn't expect to be here, Brian wanted to say.

"So, this is your new job," Don said with a smirk. "Suits you. All this sweet and fancy stuff."

"What can I get you guys?" he asked, tamping down his own humiliation.

Don pulled a face as he looked around the display cases, then the bread racks. "You out of doughnuts already?" He shook his head, tut-tutting. "You snoozing standing up?"

Brian recognized the comment as a jab he gave Don from time to time when Brian found him slacking off. His back stiffened but he knew he couldn't let this guy get to him.

"I doubt that. Melissa said we were well stocked." But he walked behind the display cases to make sure.

Don was right. They were out of doughnuts. Great, his first minute on the job and he had already messed up.

"I'll be back," he said.

Melissa was cracking eggs into a large mixing bowl on a stand.

"We're out of doughnuts," he said, unable to keep his annoyance with Don out of his voice.

Melissa brushed some dough off her chin with her shoulder, then frowned at him. "We're not out of doughnuts because I don't make them."

"What? Really?"

"No. I thought I would try a different direction with the bakery." She hit a switch and the huge paddle of the mixing bowl started spinning around.

Brian could only stare at her. "Everyone expects doughnuts at a bakery. That's not a good direction."

Melissa's expression darkened. "I think I know best what I'm trying to accomplish in my own bakery."

Now she was getting all uppity with him. One of those "her way or the highway" bosses. He'd worked under a couple of them in the factory.

He also knew sometimes you just needed to push.

"I'm sure you do, but the other bakery we had here always had doughnuts."

"And where is that bakery now?" Not hard to hear the chill in her voice as she turned the mixer off.

Brian just stared at her, then spun around and walked away. "No doughnuts today," he said to Don. "But I got some amazing 'petty fours' you could try." He couldn't keep the sarcasm out of his voice.

"Nah. I prefer something I can bite into. Guess you don't get our business today," Don said, tossing off a wave. "Don't get your apron dirty."

Brian drew in a slow breath as he watched

them leave. Just fantastic. Now it would be all over town. Brian Montclair wore an apron. A pink-and-white-striped apron.

Awesome.

But now it was quiet in the bakery and he needed to do something. He walked over to the wooden shelves and straightened the loaves of bread. Once he was done with that, he glanced down at the floor, noticing the crumbs there. Guess Melissa and Amanda were too busy baking to clean up. He strode to the back of the bakery, looking for cleaning supplies.

Melissa was dividing some of the mixture she had made over a set of four baking pans sitting on a scale. "Something I can help you with?" she asked as she looked up from what she was doing.

"Nope," he replied, still fuming at Don's "lady boss" comment and Melissa's previous attitude to his suggestions.

He grabbed a broom and dustpan from the cleaning supply room and walked past Melissa without a glance her way.

He swept the floor in the front, again taking out his frustration with a broom. *What kind of bakery doesn't carry doughnuts?* City girl and her fancy cakes and pastries that cost too much. Not so good for business in a town where people were struggling to get by.

He made short work of cleaning the floor, then strode to the back again, returned the broom and came back with a spray bottle of window cleaner. He wiped down the front of the display cases, surprised at how many fingermarks were on it. Wasn't Amanda supposed to take care of this?

Guess it was his job now.

The rest of the day went by with fits and starts of work. Some people came in to simply look, a few more to buy. He wasn't terribly busy, but he wasn't too bored.

But as he worked he was far too aware of the woman fussing away in the bakery behind him.

Just get over it, he thought.

By the time the day was over, his feet were sore from standing on the concrete floor and his temper hadn't improved much. He had to keep reminding himself why he was doing this. For Grandpa.

Sunday was a relaxing day. He and Grandpa walked around the yard, making a few plans, reminding Brian again of why he was putting on a fancy apron come Monday. Next weekend they were going to Concordia to move his stuff back here.

When he arrived at the job Monday morning, Melissa wasn't working at the large butcher block counter, nor was she in her office. He followed the sound of a machine and found her in the back of the bakery twisting a bag of bread and clipping it shut.

She started when he came in. "What's that?" he asked, pointing to the machine.

"Bread slicer."

"How does it work?"

She frowned at him as she set the bagged bread on a large rack already holding a number of loaves and plucked another unsliced loaf from the rack on the other side. "I guess you could learn how to run this," she said as she dropped it into a slot on the top of the machine. It wasn't too hard to hear the reluctance in her voice.

Control freak, he thought again.

"I guess I could," he returned. "Not much happening right now."

She shot him a frown, as if she wasn't sure what to make of his comment, then, to his surprise, stepped aside. "You set the bread here, push this button, wait until it comes into this chute and slip a bag over top. Hit the release button and then twist the top and put a clip on."

Brian followed her instructions, the noise of the machine precluding any other conversation, crumbs flying from the blades cutting the bread. A few seconds later he had a bag of bread closed off and ready to put on the rack.

"Good," she said, sounding surprised that he had caught on so quickly. "That's good."

"I'll do the rest," he said, setting the loaf on the rack and grabbing another one. "You go bake some petty fours."

She looked like she was about to protest, then with a shrug, she turned, leaving him to his job.

The work was tedious, but it kept him busy and soon he had all the loaves done and was wheeling the full rack to the front of the bakery.

As he set the loaves neatly on the shelves, the door opened again and their first customers of the day stepped into the bakery. Brian turned to see a young woman and little girl enter. He tried not to flush as he recognized Lexi Ross, a girl he had dated in high school. Her long blond hair, green eyes and narrow features had made her the darling of Bygones and the epitome of Midwest wholesomeness. Now she and her husband, Wilson Ross, lived with their three children in a two-story Victorian off Granary Road.

Lexi gave him an awkward smile as she glanced from him to his apron to the loaf of bread he still held. How the mighty have fallen, he thought, remembering how he used to tell her he would one day be his own boss, run his own business.

"What can I help you with?" he asked, unable to keep the gruff note out of his voice.

Treena Ross, six years old, her short blond hair like dandelion fluff around her round face, looked up at him, then back at her mother. Her lower lip quivered and her green eyes welled up with tears. "He scares me, mom," she said. "Why is that big man working here?"

Lexi gave Brian an apologetic grin, then crouched beside her daughter, her full skirt brushing the floor. Her hair fell over her face as she bent her head toward her daughter, lowering her voice to assure her. "He's a nice man. That's Mr. Montclair. You saw him yesterday at our church, remember? Now why don't you ask Mr. Montclair what you came here to do?"

Treena sniffed, palmed her tears off her cheek then held up a piece of paper. "Can you sign my perdition?" she asked in a small voice. "I want the school to stay open so I can go there. Like my mommy and daddy did."

Brian frowned as he took the paper from the little girl. "What do you mean, stay open?"

Lexi brushed Treena's hair away from her face and gave Brian a despondent look. "We got a letter from the county school board saying she and her brother, Phil, will be bussed to Concordia School, over an hour away, when school starts. They are thinking of closing down the school here in Bygones."

"Close down the school? Why?"

"Budget cutbacks," Lexi said. "They don't think they have enough money to keep it open this year."

Brian fought his frustration and anger. What was happening to his town? Why were things going so badly?

He looked at the little girl, trying to imagine her sitting on a bus for more than an hour instead of walking to school like so many children in Bygones did. As a kid he used to take the school bus, but in the summertime he and his sisters would bike from their home on the edge of town, enjoying the freedom of their own transportation.

"I'll sign your petition, Treena." He pushed himself to his feet and pulled a pen out of a jar sitting by the cash register. He scribbled his signature, then handed the paper back to Treena. "I hope the school doesn't get closed down. Let me know what happens, Lexi," he said as he straightened.

"What's going on?"

Melissa stood behind him, a frown puckering her forehead, her arms folded over her chest.

And why was she frowning at him now?

"Lexi and Treena wanted me to sign a petition

but I'll get right back to work," he said with a hint of asperity. Before she could say anything he grabbed the empty bread rack and pushed it, wheels squeaking in protest, to the back to finish his job.

Melissa watched Brian go, biting back a sigh. His second day on the job and he still exuded resentment. This was not going well. Saturday she had hoped to talk to Dale Eversleigh about helping her with another list of prospective employees and then Brian came walking into the bakery. For a moment she had been tempted to rescind her job offer, but she didn't dare. She was the newcomer to Bygones and the SOS Committee held the strings and dictated the terms of her loan.

So she had, very reluctantly, hired him. And, it seemed, he was just as reluctant to work here, which made her wonder why he took the job.

She wasn't sure whether she needed to talk to him about his attitude or wait and see if it changed. At least he knew how to work. She was still surprised he had cleaned up the front so well on Saturday and was willing to learn how to bag bread today.

As she turned her attention back to the little girl named Treena, she thought of how kind

Brian had been to her. He was a puzzling study in contrasts, that's for sure.

"What did Mr. Montclair mean when he said he hoped the school didn't close down?" she asked.

Treena held up her paper again. "I have a perdition here—"

"Petition," Lexi corrected as Melissa stifled a quick smile.

"Petition," the little girl corrected. "I thought people in town could help me and sign my paper. Maybe I could give it to the school board and they would change their mind."

Melissa glanced at Lexi, who gave her a "what can I do?" smile. "It was her idea so I said I would accompany her to the various businesses. It can't hurt."

"Of course I'll sign," Melissa said. As she added her name and signature to the paper, she noticed Brian's above hers. His writing was a large, dark scrawl.

Not unlike the man himself, she thought, giving the girl her paper back. "I hope that helps," she said with a rueful look.

Lexi placed her hand on her daughter's shoulder. "I do, too. A six-year-old shouldn't have to sit on the bus for over an hour to get to school." She gave Melissa a quick smile, then glanced over at the display case. "While we're here, I'd like to try some of the new pastries I've heard some rave reviews about."

Melissa's heart warmed at the compliment. "Sure. What would you like?"

"I can deal with the customers."

Brian's gruff voice behind her gave her a start, but she shook her head. "No. That's okay. I don't mind." She turned back to Lexi.

Lexi glanced from Brian to Melissa as if unsure who to talk to.

"I want a doughnut," Treena piped up, obviously not caring who she needed to deal with.

"Sorry, honey. I don't have any doughnuts," Melissa said.

"Wow. They must be amazing if you're out already," Lexi said.

"I don't carry doughnuts."

Lexi looked taken aback and Melissa could almost feel Brian's smirk behind her.

"I'm aiming for a different product line," Melissa said, trying not to sound defensive. "Something less traditional."

"Okay. Then I'll have a half-dozen white chocolate blueberry scones and a dozen toffee crunch cookies."

"Coming right up." Melissa turned to put on her plastic disposable gloves and almost ran into Brian standing right behind her, gloves already on.

"I said I'll take care of this," he growled. "You go bake your little fours or whatever you call them."

She held his steady gaze, his eyebrows lowered over his deep-set eyes, and felt the tiniest frisson of fear. Then she dismissed it. She would not be intimidated by an employee, but at the same time she sensed he was not backing down.

"Okay. I'll be in the back," she said with a forced smile, knowing she would have to talk to him later about the boss/employee relationship. If he was going to work here, they needed to keep a few things straight.

After Lexi and Treena left, the bell rang again and a group of people came in. Melissa heard laughter, Brian's gruff response and more laughter.

She was curious but stayed where she was, not sure she wanted to deal with Brian's grumpiness any more than she had to.

Quiet ensued, but then another group of people came in. Sounded like women from the voices. More laughter. Melissa knew she should keep her concentration on the new recipe she was working on for Mrs. Morgan.

She corrected a few of the amounts, but her inquisitiveness got the better of her and she stepped away from her table, peeking around the corner to see the front of the store.

Two women stood by the display cases, quizzing Brian about the products and teasing him.

"I guess your Home Ec classes are finally getting put to good use," one of the women, a tall brunette, was saying. She fingered her long hair, giving Brian a flirtatious look.

"I just got a job here because I kneaded the dough," he said with a wry tone in his voice. Melissa pressed down a giggle at his unexpected humor, but neither of the women seemed to catch the double entendre.

"I never thought I'd see the day a woman put an apron on the rough, tough Brian Montclair," the other woman said, her green eyes flashing behind a pair of heavy rimmed glasses, her hair a mass of dark curls springing away from her narrow face.

"Now, now, Anita, I'm not that helpless. I put this apron on all by myself," he said, joining in on their laughter.

"So is this your new calling?" Anita asked, wrapping her arms around her narrow frame, giving Brian a flirtatious look. "Baking cupcakes and squares?"

"I don't care to do any of the girlie baking stuff," Brian returned. "That's Miss—"

"City Slicker's job," Anita finished for him. "I heard you call her that after the Grand Opening. After all the grumbling you did there about the new businesses I never thought I'd see you working at one of them."

"Well, as Miss Coraline always said, the Lord moves in mysterious ways. His wonders to perform," Brian returned with a tight smile. "Speaking of wonders, Trudy, you have to try this apple pastry."

"I'll take half a dozen," Trudy replied.

"Only half? Your husband and kids will have half of them eaten before Sunday comes around," he said, putting six more in another box.

"Always were a smooth talker," Anita said, adding a wink. "Have you been turning your charm on the owner of the bakery, Miss Melissa City Slicker? She's single. Pretty. She reminds me of Tracy, one of your many old girlfriends."

Melissa knew she should get back to work, but for some reason she was suddenly curious about Brian's romantic history.

"Miss City Slicker is nothing like Tracy," Brian retorted.

His cutting words bothered her more than she cared to admit, as did the mention of many old girlfriends, but just as she was about to go back to her recipe, he turned.

Their eyes held a moment and, in spite of his caustic tone and in spite of what he had said about her, she couldn't look away.

For a moment she had felt a flicker of jealousy
that these women could elicit what she couldn't.
A genuine smile.

Chapter Four

"Brian, can you come to the back a moment? I just got the strangest letter," Melissa called out.

It was Tuesday afternoon, his third day on the job, and though the work still was uncomfortable to him, he felt like he was getting a handle on things.

This morning he had bagged bread again and had cleaned up the bread mixer. The morning hadn't been really busy, but business had been steady.

"What could you possibly have received in the mail that has anything to do with me?" he asked, looking up from the full cookie tray he had just set in the display case. He brushed his hands over his apron as he straightened. Melissa's frown deepened and Brian knew he had stepped over the line again. Didn't seem hard to do with his new boss.

"According to this letter, I'm supposed to read this aloud to you and Amanda," she said.

With a shrug of resignation Brian followed her to the back part of the bakery.

Amanda stood by the smaller mixer, measuring flour into the batter. When she looked up from what she was doing, her expressions was as confused as Brian's.

"So what's up, Melissa?" she asked, turning off the mixer and going to the sink to wash her hands. "What's with the mini meeting back here?"

"I got a letter from the benefactor, the person with all the money. It came yesterday. I'm supposed to read it to you both." She cleared her throat, took a breath and began.

"Dear Melissa, Amanda and Brian—"

"He or she knows who is working here?" Brian interrupted. "I only started Saturday. That's creepy."

"Maybe he or she is part of the SOS Committee," Melissa said with a shrug.

Brian doubted that. Who on the committee would have access to the kind of money this person had been throwing around? Mr. Randall? If he did, why didn't he put that money into the factory?

"'Melissa, congratulations on your new venture and the work that you've done so far,'"

Melissa continued, resting her hip against the butcher block work counter. "'I want to encourage you as you try to expand the scope of the bakery and find ways to bring new business to our town.'"

Melissa wrinkled her nose at that comment. "Easier said than done, Mysterious Benefactor," she muttered.

"Doughnuts would help," Brian said, folding his arms over his chest.

Melissa shot him a caustic look.

"Seriously, about one third of the customers who've come in the past couple of days have asked about doughnuts."

"I'm aware of the lack of doughnuts. I used to serve the customers, too."

"Just sayin'," he said, holding up his hand.

"Always sayin'," she returned.

Brian held her steady gaze, wondering why she had hired him. Of course, it wasn't like he was the most willing employee.

I do my work, he reminded himself.

Melissa returned to her letter, then paused, tapping her finger against her lip. Then she shot Brian a puzzled glance that held a hint of humor.

Now what?

"'Brian, it wouldn't hurt for you to lighten up a little. Smile occasionally. Working in a bakery isn't only for women. There's a long history of famous chefs and bakers being men.'"

"You're making that up, City Slicker," Brian snorted.

"It says it right here," Melissa returned, holding the letter toward him, her eyes narrowing at his City Slicker dig. "You can read it for yourself."

Brian waved off the offer, though he was sorely tempted. "I'll believe you."

"Whoever wrote it is right," Amanda said, tossing the towel she used to dry her hands over her shoulder, her blue eyes piercing him. "You're not always so nice to Melissa."

Brian didn't reply to that. Melissa wasn't always so nice to Brian either.

"Moving along," Melissa said. "'Melissa, I want to commend you on making such a drastic change from baking at a hotel in the big city of St. Louis to your own bakery in the small town of Bygones. Amanda, you're doing good work, but it is important to show up to a job on time.'"

Amanda reared back. "Who is this guy? Santa Claus keeping track of who's been naughty and nice?"

"How do you know it's a guy?" Melissa said. "Could be a woman."

"It's got to be someone from the town. Someone who's been in the bakery," Amanda said.

"That's not been many people," Brian replied, thinking of how quiet the bakery had been this morning. He'd spent half of his time cleaning up and tidying the storage room holding the bulk supplies.

"It's picking up," Melissa said, sounding defensive. "That's why I hired you."

"Even Ellen Langston stopped in to buy some of Melissa's tarts this morning," Amanda said, leaping to Melissa's defense like a mother hen defending her chicks. "And one time I heard her saying there was no way she would set foot in here when she could bake herself."

"Good for her," Brian returned, crossing his arms over his chest. "But it's still been quiet."

Melissa pursed her lips at his comment. Brian just shrugged. Nothing he could do about the facts. He kept busy, but business wasn't exactly booming. He wondered if Melissa would be able to keep him hired.

The thought sent a sliver of dread through him. Though this job hadn't been his first choice, it was a paycheck that he needed right now.

"Maybe it's Miss Ann Mars who has all the money," Amanda said.

Brian shook his head. "Doubtful. She can't make that much selling secondhand goods."

"She could be, you know, like, a miser?"

Amanda said. "I saw someone like that on a TV show. They lived like they were all poor and stuff but they had a box full of money shoved under a board in the floor of a room."

Brian shrugged. "A miser wouldn't be throwing money around like this person has. Besides, Ann Mars is far from a miser and you know it, Amanda True."

"Maybe Miss Coraline," Amanda persisted. "Maybe she inherited a bunch of money no one knows about."

"That's a lot of money to keep secret."

Brian didn't want to know who handed out the money. If it was someone he knew, he was afraid he would have a target for the resentment that clawed at him from time to time. He still didn't understand why out-of-towners like Miss City Slicker here got chosen over someone like him who knew Bygones and the people who lived here.

He dragged his hand over his face, as if to erase the emotions. Until his mechanic work took off, he didn't have much else going on in his life.

"There's no sense trying to figure out who handed out the money," Brian continued. "He or she seemed to have some strange ideas who to give it to."

Melissa shot him a frown and looked like she

wanted to say something when the bell over the door announced a new customer, giving Brian the perfect reason to leave the back room and let Amanda and Melissa get back to their work.

Whitney Leigh, reporter for the *Gazette,* Bygones's official newspaper, stood just inside the bakery, her bright eyes behind her glasses flitting around the room as if looking for something she wasn't finding, her bun like a tight knot at the nape of her neck. She had a camera bag slung over one shoulder and a tape recorder in her hand. Her tailored blazer and narrow skirt looked out of place in a town where most people wore the first thing they grabbed out of the closet, but Whitney liked to look put together. In charge. In control.

"Hey, Brian," Whitney said when her eyes alighted on him. "I heard you were working here."

"Hardly worth putting in your paper," he said, unable to keep the prickly note out of his voice. He could already see the potential picture and accompanying article. Brian Montclair, former mechanic, now baker, complete with pink-striped apron. "What can I do for you?"

"I'd like to talk to Melissa."

"What about?"

Whitney shrugged. "Just some questions about Mr. Moneybags."

Brian turned to get Melissa from the back where she was working with Amanda, but she already stood behind him, still holding the envelope containing the letter.

"What can I help you with?" Melissa asked, slipping the letter inside the pocket of her apron.

"Just a few questions. I'm doing an ongoing series on Mr. Moneybags—?"

"Who?" Brian asked.

Whitney raised her hand as she took a few steps closer.

"The mysterious benefactor. The guy with the bags of money," she said with a shrug. "I'm doing an investigative piece for the *Gazette*."

"I'm afraid I can't help you," Melissa said. "And I'm not from around here, so I can't even begin to speculate."

"Then I'd like to ask you what made you decide to come to Bygones."

"It was the opportunity to start a new business. Something I've always wanted to do."

Brian was surprised to hear the pleasure in Melissa's voice, the satisfaction in her smile.

"And you were given no indication of who the money came from that helped you start this business?"

Melissa shook her head. "Only that it was administered through the SOS Committee, that I had to commit to staying for two years and that

I had to hire locals from Bygones. But I had no idea who held the purse strings."

Which is how he got this amazing job, Brian thought.

At least it was work, he reminded himself. Grandpa was happier than he'd been in years.

Whitney tapped her lower lip with one manicured finger, as if thinking. "I don't know why Mr. Moneybags is so secretive. Which makes me even more curious." She flashed Brian and Melissa a grin. "One way or the other, I'm figuring out who this person is."

"Why does it matter?" Brian asked. "Maybe he wants to keep his generosity a secret. Maybe your Mr. Moneybags is Ms. Moneybags."

"Could it be Mr. Randall?" Melissa put in. "The man who owns the factory?"

Whitney shook her head. "He said no, but he's always been a cagey one."

"I think we can count him out," Brian said. "Now that the factory is closed down."

Whitney eased up one shoulder in a vague shrug. "I heard Randall might be looking for alternate financing. That he might be opening up again."

Expectation surged through Brian at her words, igniting the faint hope he'd been nurturing since he got this job. "Did he say when?"

Whitney shook her head. "How do you like

working here, Brian?" Whitney asked, obviously realizing that finding out the identity of Mr. Moneybags was a dead end.

"It's work," Brian said with a shrug. He didn't want to discuss his employment situation with Whitney. Who knows what she would put in her article. She loved to stir the pot.

"Who would have thought that a guy who I heard could build a car from the ground up would be making pastries?" Whitney returned, still digging.

"I'm a man of many talents," Brian said dryly.

Whitney held his gaze a moment longer, as if hoping to get something else from him, then turned back to Melissa. "I'd love to buy something but maybe another time. I'm on a deadline right now." Whitney tucked her recorder back in her pocket. "If you think of anything or hear anything about this secret backer, let me know. I'll find who this Mr. Moneybags is one way or the other, but I wouldn't mind some help." Before either Brian or Melissa could reply she strode out of the bakery, a woman on a mission.

"Did you get one of those letters?" Lily set her steaming cappuccino down on the table where Melissa sat at Josh's coffee shop and plopped into the chair beside her. "From the person with all the money?"

It was Tuesday evening and the first meeting of the newly formed Shopkeepers Society, something the SOS Committee, with their love for alliteration, had come up with. Josh—owner of the Cozy Cup Café, the coffee shop—Lily—owner of Love in Bloom—and Melissa were three of the shopkeepers represented at the meeting.

The other members were Patrick Fogerty, proprietor of The Fixer-Upper; Allison True, Amanda's sister, who ran the bookshop; and Chase Rollins, the owner of Fluff & Stuff, a pet store.

"I did. Felt kind of creepy how much this person knows about us. You should have seen Brian's face when I read the part about him not being so cranky," Melissa said.

"That letter said that?" Lily's mouth dropped open in shock, her wavy blond hair swinging around her face. "Wow. I imagine that didn't go over well with Grumpy Gus."

"It certainly didn't."

"How has he been behaving?"

Melissa shrugged, not sure what to say. "He's a good salesman and charming with the customers. Just not so charming with me."

Lilly gave her a curious grin. "I'm sensing that bothers you more than you care to admit?"

Melissa shrugged off Lily's probing question, pressing her finger against the faint headache that had been threatening all afternoon. "I've heard enough negative comments about the need for a bakery when people could make most of what I offer for half of the price of what I charge. I don't need, on top of that, to have an employee who doesn't like me and keeps bugging me to make doughnuts." Melissa tossed the words out in what she hoped was a casual tone, but deep down Brian's smoldering resentment bothered her in a way she didn't want to analyze too deeply.

"I think Brian's frustrated," Lily said. "Tate told me Brian had applied to the SOS Committee for money for a mechanic shop and, obviously, had been turned down. Maybe that's why he's resentful."

Melissa frowned. "I didn't know that."

"As outsiders there's lots we don't know about this town or the people in it yet," Lily said with a quick smile. "It might help if you let Brian know you feel bad about him not getting approved."

Melissa was saved from answering by Coraline clapping her hands to get everyone's attention.

Still a teacher, thought Melissa, turning in her chair.

Coraline stood at one end of the coffee shop. She was dressed in a blue suit, her white shirt setting off the gray sheen of her hair. "I want to thank you all for coming out to this shopkeepers' meeting, and special thanks to Josh for hosting it. I think we should go to the bakery next time. Every time I go by I smell these amazing aromas," Coraline said, turning her charm on Melissa.

Melissa simply smiled, not sure what she was supposed to say, then Miss Coraline carried on.

"Tonight I want to discuss expectations and initiatives. I thought we could brainstorm ideas for not only rejuvenating Bygones, as was the expectation attached to the grant money, but also for drawing customers from outside Bygones. Has anyone come up with anything they'd like to share? Some idea they would like to implement in their own business?"

A few people made some comments and some ideas were thrown around, but Melissa, to her shame, couldn't come up with anything.

Miss Coraline glanced at her, as if hoping she would have some ideas to contribute, but Melissa only gave her a sheepish smile.

"I'd like to know if anyone else got a letter from our mystery benefactor this week," Chase Rollins, the owner of Fluff & Stuff spoke up, his deep voice commanding everyone's attention. He looked around the room, a frown making his brown eyes look even darker.

"I am not sure what you are talking about," Coraline said. "What letter?"

"From the coffee shop buzz, it seems all the owners of the new businesses got a letter from this backer, encouraging them in their ventures," Josh said, folding his arms over his chest and tilting back in his chair.

"Whoever wrote it seemed to know a lot about us," Alison True put in. "He or she knew that I used to live here."

"And that I used to have a hardware store in Michigan," Patrick Fogerty put in.

"I'm sorry. I don't know enough about this letter to address your questions," Coraline said, raising her hand to stem the sudden buzz of conversation. "I prefer to discuss what we have on the agenda."

Her unwillingness to discuss the letter made Melissa wonder if she was the one who wrote it. Very curious.

The talk moved from who the benefactor could be to discussing ideas for expanding their business and their struggles with gaining trust and acceptance from the other members of the town. The meeting went on for another few minutes but then wound down. Melissa was about to ask Lily if she wanted another coffee when her friend suddenly shot a look at her watch.

"Sorry," she said to Melissa. "I have to run. Isabella wanted me to read her a bedtime story tonight."

Melissa nodded, feeling a nudge of self-pity as she watched Lily leave, her eyes shining with expectation. Lily looked so happy.

When Lily first came to Bygones, Tate Bronson had been the one to pick her up from the airport and bring her to the town. When Lily met Tate's seven-year-old daughter, Isabella, the two of them had immediately connected. But Tate's grief over the loss of his wife had created a distance between him and Lily. However, Lily's sweetness and kindness had breached that gulf.

Every time Melissa saw Lily and Tate together, she wondered if she would ever find that kind of love.

She thought she had found it with Jason but knew the relationship to be a hollow version of what she was looking for. She wanted someone who would put her first.

Melissa felt a tap on her shoulder and turned to see Miss Coraline standing in front of her, her handbag tucked over one arm. "What did you think of the meeting?" she asked.

Melissa gave a noncommittal shrug. "I think it went well."

"Some of the shopkeepers have some interesting ideas to bring in other business." Coraline gave Melissa an encouraging smile, as if hoping that in a one-on-one situation, Melissa might be willing to share her own ideas.

"Sorry I couldn't contribute," Melissa said with an apologetic smile. "I know I'm no less of an outsider than the other business owners, but I'm not sure where to start with bringing in other business other than the couple of contacts I've created with hotels in Junction City."

"Of course, my dear. It's hard enough just keeping your business going without thinking of all the other things required by the committee." Coraline touched her lower lip, frowning slightly, as if dredging up her own ideas. "You might want to talk to Brian. Maybe he might have some suggestions."

Melissa almost choked on her coffee. "Brian is the most taciturn employee I've seen," she sputtered. "I can't imagine he wants to talk with me about the bakery."

"Brian may not have chosen the job he's been given," Coraline said, the faint note of reprimand in her voice making Melissa feel guilty, "but he's a good person underneath all that gruffness and bluster. Maybe if you ask him, you might get him more invested in the business. Might give him a sense that he's needed."

Melissa's only reply was a light nod, trying to imagine what, if anything, Brian could bring to the business and whether he cared or not. "I'll think on that" was all she could say.

"That's all I ask you to do."

Melissa gathered her purse and coffee and nodded at Patrick. A sudden pain shot through her head. She groaned as she pushed open the door of Josh's coffee shop, stepping into the warm evening air.

She hoped she wasn't coming down with a migraine. She didn't get them often, but when she did, she was almost incapacitated.

As she was walking past the Dill's store, The Everything, she paused, as she always did, by the community billboard. Papers flapped in the evening breeze announcing items for sale from people moving out of town. The number of pieces of furniture, appliances, children's toys and bicycles still for sale was depressing. A précis of the still-ongoing exodus of people from Bygones, Melissa thought, skimming over the ads.

A bright yellow paper with black writing caught her eye. She hadn't seen it yesterday and, curious, she began reading.

Need mechanic work done? Can do trucks, cars, motorcycles and some large equipment. Call for quotes. Brian Montclair.

Melissa was surprised at the displeasure the notice gave her. It was sort of like someone applying for a job while still working for you. As if she wasn't paying enough.

She stifled her annoyance as she turned and strode down the cracked sidewalk, past The Everything and cutting across Bronson Street by the school. What Brian did in his spare time was none of her business. Of course he could run a mechanic business on the side. It shouldn't matter to her. She knew Brian only took the job at the bakery because he had to and because nothing else was available.

As long as he showed up every day, ready to work at her bakery, she shouldn't care what else he did when he wasn't working for her.

But deep down she did.

Chapter Five

"Anything you need me to do?" Brian stood in the back of the bakery watching as Melissa dropped a large rectangular slab of cake on the counter in front of her.

Melissa shook her head. "Bread went out this morning to the store and the next thing would be this cake. Why?"

"I don't want to leave for lunch until Amanda comes and I'm done with all my other work." The bread was sliced, the floor around it was cleaned up and the display cases shone. The walk-in freezer was organized as was the refrigerator.

"I'm okay…" Melissa hesitated as she clung to the edge of the table.

"You're crazy busy is what you are and you hired me to help. Let me help."

Melissa shot him a wry look. "I need icing made."

He frowned. "I don't know how to do that."

"Then I guess, unless you're willing do girlie baking stuff and make icing, there's not much else I can get you to do."

Brian felt his back stiffen. He knew how his comment of the other day sounded and how his current reluctance looked, but he also knew Melissa prided herself on perfection. Amanda often grumbled about Melissa not letting her do much hands-on work, and he didn't want to mess things up.

At the same time, he felt as if she was issuing him a challenge. "I'm supposed to be some kind of assistant. If you don't mind how it turns out, I'll make your frosting," he returned.

"Don't worry, I'll tell you exactly what to do," she said.

"Don't you always," he muttered.

"That is part of my job," she said, dropping her hand on her hip in a challenging gesture. "I am your boss, after all."

"Yeah. I got that." As soon as the grumble left his lips he regretted, again, what he'd said.

It was their situation, he told himself. He had been a boss in charge of guys. He didn't like having the situation switched on him like this. Like an itch he couldn't scratch, the fact that he was the bottom of the totem pole in this bakery, the fact that Melissa was his boss, was a constant reminder of how far he had fallen. And how far he had fallen from his dream of being his own boss and having his own family.

How could he support anyone on what he made?

The Lord opposes the proud, but shows favor to the humble.

The quote from James echoed in his mind, reminding him of what he needed to do, and he eased out a light sigh.

"So what do I start with?" he said.

"Ten pounds of shortening and ten pounds of butter in the mixer," she said. "The paddle is already on the mixer so just cream it once you've got the butter and shortening in it."

"Got it."

When Brian came back from the cooler with the butter, he saw Melissa leaning over on the counter, her head down.

"You okay?" he asked. "You don't look good."

"Just what every woman needs to hear."

"It's the truth."

"I just have a headache," she said as she walked over to the magnetic strip holding an array of knives and spatulas.

Her snippy tone grated on him. He was showing her concern. Guess she didn't want any from him.

"Okay, Miss City Slicker," he conceded, dumping the shortening and butter into the large stainless steel mixing bowl. He looked for the power button and turned it on.

He knew he pushed *her* buttons with his City Slicker comment, but the past couple of days he couldn't stop thinking about her and didn't like that feeling.

Like he had told his friend Anita when she visited the bakery, Melissa was nothing like Tracy, his former girlfriend. Melissa was a hard worker. She was here well before he arrived every morning and often stayed past closing time. The guys who used to work for him at the factory could take notes from her on work ethic and dedication.

But Brian knew who he was. Her employee. Nothing more. Just like she had reminded him a few moments ago.

The buzzer rang announcing a customer so he washed his hands, skirted the mixer and walked to the front of the store. He couldn't help a quick glance Melissa's way. She was slicing the cakes into two slabs with a large, thin knife but her face was the color of the cake she was working with.

She didn't look good, but since he had started working for Melissa, one thing he had found out loud and clear was that she didn't like being fussed over or having undue attention drawn to herself. So he said nothing and went to the front to attend to the customers.

When he came back, Amanda had finally arrived and was dumping some yellow stuff into the mixer holding the frosting, Melissa calling out instructions.

Guess Melissa didn't need his help after all. He glanced at the clock. 12:30. Now that Amanda was here he could take his break.

"I'm going for lunch," Brian said, yanking off his apron and hanging it on the hook at the back of the store. As he pulled his sandwiches out of the fridge, he turned to see Melissa draw in a long breath, lifting her shoulder to swipe at a bead of sweat slipping down the side of her flushed face.

"You look like you could take a break, too," he said, concerned at how she looked.

Melissa shook her head. "Mrs. Morgan is coming at 2:00 to do some sampling."

"Amanda can cover everything here."

"Not really. I need to get this cake iced and then start up on another batch of pies."

Brian was about to tell her to get Amanda to help her but then the buzzer sounded. He reached for his apron but Amanda held her hand up to stop him. "I'll take care of the customers."

Guess he wasn't needed here. So he headed

out the back door to Bronson Park to have his lunch in the warm summer sunshine.

All by himself. Just the way he liked it.

"Someone here to see you," Amanda called out, walking into the back of the bakery.

"Who is it?" Melissa finished the last of the roses she was piping on the first layer of the cake and blinked. Everything was blurry. What was wrong with her eyes?

"Dale Eversleigh from the funeral home," Amanda said with a grin, her blue eyes flashing with fun. "You're not *that* sick, are you?"

"I'm not sick." Melissa's denial was negated by a sharp pain slicing through her head. "Tell him I'll be right out."

Mr. Eversleigh stood in the front of the bakery, twisting his hands around each other, his blond toupee looking even more artificial under the lights of the bakery. Today his outfit was more subdued, his gray suit a change from the garish plaid coats and brightly colored pants he seemed to prefer when he wasn't working. Melissa guessed he must have come here directly from the funeral home.

"Can I help you, Mr. Eversleigh?" she asked.

"I'm here to help you," Dale said, giving her a bright, overly friendly smile that, she suspected, he had perfected over many years of working at the funeral home. "And you can call me Dale. I had some free time and thought I would stop in to see how you are doing."

Why was everyone so concerned about her health? "I'm fine. Just fine, thanks. All this fresh, small-town air."

Even as she spoke the words her conscience and the headache dogging her all morning accused her. She wasn't fine. Her head pounded and she felt as if she was walking in a fog. She was surprised Brian had noticed and was as surprised at the faint note of concern she'd heard in his voice.

"Actually, you misunderstood," he said, his ingratiating smile deepening, his gold tooth winking back at her. "I'm a member of the SOS Committee that set up the funding for your business. I was hoping to spend a few moments chatting about the business. Wondering if you needed any tips, business help, that sort of thing." His smile deepened and Melissa couldn't help but remember how Lily had warned her about Dale "hitting" on her.

But meeting with her SOS contact was part of the loan requirements so, ignoring her increasingly pounding head and her second thoughts about spending too much time alone with Dale, she smiled and nodded in agreement.

"Of course. Would you like to go to the coffee shop across the street?"

Dale shook his head. "It's far too busy there and I spend enough time indoors. If you don't mind, could we go to the park?"

She wanted to resist, guessing that Brian was probably having his lunch in the park, but she didn't have the strength or will to change the plans.

"Would you like to have something from the bakery for lunch?" she offered.

He shook his head and added another excessively friendly smile. "No. I'm trying to watch my weight," he said, patting his rounded stomach. "You go ahead."

"I ate already," she said. Half a muffin at about ten o'clock, but she didn't feel like discussing her eating habits with Dale.

Her stomach had felt queasy all morning, and after the muffin she didn't want to risk eating and feeling worse. "We may as well go out through the back of the bakery to the park. That way I can show you the bakery equipment as we go."

"Sounds good," he said.

As they walked through the back Melissa pointed out the work station, bread proofer, oven and storage rooms, unable to keep the pride out of her voice. Dale nodded with each explanation but Melissa saw by his vague smile and quick glances that he was simply humoring her. Maybe if there was a dead body in the freezer he might be interested.

As they stepped out the back door, the bright sun almost blinded Melissa. As usual she had been awake before the sun came up and working inside ever since. It wasn't often she stepped outside during the day.

Some kind of life you chose for yourself, girl.

She brushed the cynical thought aside, reminding herself that she owned her own business. This was something she had dreamed of from the first moment she applied for her baking classes at the community college.

She and Mr. Eversleigh walked across the street, the heat of the sun beating down from the sky and rising from the black pavement. The green grass and shady trees of Bronson Park beckoned like an oasis.

They walked along a path through the tall trees toward the picnic benches. Children's laughter echoed from the park beyond the gazebo.

Lily, who must have been on a break from her flower shop next door, got up from a park bench and waved Melissa over, her fingers fluttering like the petals of a flower. "Are you finally taking a break?" she teased, shaking crumbs from her lacy pink dress. "I haven't seen you for so long."

"Business is picking up, so I've been working more."

"How lovely to see you, Lily," Dale said, his grin flicking from Melissa to Lily. "I hope you've been satisfied with the business I've managed to acquire for you."

"Quite pleased, though I'm sad for the reason," Lily said, turning to Melissa and giving her the barest of winks. "We'll have to book some time for coffee and a long gossip instead of the bits and pieces of conversation we've tossed each other on the fly."

"How are Tate and Isabella?" Melissa asked.

Lily gave Melissa a coy smile, her cornflower-blue eyes shining behind her glasses. "Tate is talking about adding onto the house at the ranch," she said with a sweet giggle. "Isabella has already chosen what she wants to wear as flower girl."

Melissa felt a twinge of envy for her friend's happiness.

"Now that we've decided on what kind of cake you want we'll have to choose how I'll decorate it," Melissa said.

"By the time you get done with Gracie Wilson's wedding, you might not want to do mine," Lily said with another grin.

Melissa almost agreed. "I doubt yours will be as complicated. That wedding cake itself is up to five tiers now, housed in its own gazebo complete with fountain."

Lily laughed as she patted Melissa on the shoulder. "No gazebo for my cake, but what you'll come up with will be perfect." Lily glanced at her watch. "Sorry. Got to run. I have my own appointment with Mrs. Morgan. Probably to talk about flowers for said gazebo. Bye, Mr. Eversleigh," she said, fluttering her hands at Dale, who was watching her go with a faintly melancholy smile.

He lost out on that one, Melissa thought with a smile.

"Sorry about that," Melissa said to Dale as they walked toward the nearest empty park bench tucked in the shade of an oak tree so large it must have been here since Noah's flood. "I haven't seen Lily for a while."

"Lily is a wonderful person. We've had a number of business dealings already," Dale said, rubbing his hands together. "I'm glad to see that you two get along."

"We have a lot in common. We both came here as outsiders," Melissa replied. "Or city slickers, as Brian likes to say."

Dale laughed. "Brian can be outspoken."

"*Outspoken* isn't the word I would choose,"

she murmured as she dropped onto the bench, kicking her shoes off and letting the grass cool her feet. She had been standing all day and now her feet throbbed in time to the pounding of her head. Her legs and arms felt like limp spaghetti. It was as if the exhaustion dogging her the past few days had been waiting for her to relax before pouncing on her.

She folded her hands on the rough wood of the picnic table, the seat still cool from the shade of the huge oak tree spreading its branches over them.

"So what can I tell you about the business? What would you like to know?" she asked, forcing a perky smile to her face.

"Mostly how things are going for you financially," Dale said as he drummed his chubby fingers on the table, his pinkie ring flashing in the light. "Is the business going well?" He leaned forward a bit too close and Melissa was thankful for the space between them.

"I think business is going well." Melissa heard his questions through a growing buzz in her head and she tried to focus on what he was saying. "It's only been about a month, so it's hard to tell."

"Have you set on any plan for bringing in business from outside the community?" Dale said, reaching up to scratch his head, his toupee shifting as he did so. In spite of her throbbing head, Melissa had to smile. Guess undertaking didn't make enough to pay for a decent wig.

"Bygones is struggling financially," he continued, "And our hope was the new businesses would bring in clientele from outside the town to boost the town's revenue."

Melissa drew back even as she experienced another pang of guilt. What Dale said underlined what Coraline had said last night. "I've got a few contacts established in Concordia and I did a job for a hotel in Junction City. But it's more difficult for me given that I'm not from the area."

"That might be something you could discuss with Brian. He's well established in the community and has a number of connections."

Again he was repeating what Coraline had said, and this morning she had considered doing just that. Until she saw the poster he had put up advertising his mechanic business last night.

"I doubt he'd be much help. He only sees himself as an employee." Brian wasn't invested in the business of the bakery. To him it was a job he had to do. Reluctantly at best.

"I understand he wasn't your first choice."

"He wouldn't have been my choice at all," Melissa replied. "In fact he was last on the list. Kind of bottom of the barrel," Melissa said with a sigh, her headache making her more blunt than usual. Even as she spoke the words, she realized that wasn't what she meant. Yes, she would never have employed an unwilling person, but since he started, Brian had surprised her with his work ethic.

He kept the bakery clean and neat, constantly sweeping, washing up and organizing, making things easier for her, doing things she never asked him to do.

Dale's frown barely made a pucker in his smooth forehead. "I'm sorry to hear he's not working out for you. We can try to find someone else for you if you wish."

This was exactly what she had hoped to talk to him about earlier, but now it was too late. She was about to negate his suggestion when—

"Miss Sweeney, Miss Sweeney." A frantic voice cut into the moment. She turned to see Jack Montclair jogging across the street in her direction, waving at her. It looked like he had come from the bakery. "I'm looking for Brian," he called out.

He took a few more hurried steps across the park, then stopped at the picnic table, resting his hands on his knees to catch his breath, his face the color of strawberry jam, his white hair sticking up like chalky fingers.

The dear man looked like he was having a heart attack.

"What's the matter, Mr. Montclair?" she asked, getting up to help him. "You look all out of breath and flustered."

"Grandpa?" Brian suddenly appeared, seemingly out of nowhere, looming over Melissa and his grandfather, his hands grasping Jack's other shoulder. "What's wrong?"

Where had he come from? Had he been sitting on the other side of the tree the entire time?

Melissa's heart flopped over as the words she had spoken about him rose up like an accusation. But she couldn't deal with that. Jack was huffing and puffing beside her, clutching his chest.

"Would you like a drink?" she asked, twisting the top off the unopened bottle of water she had brought with her.

As Jack gulped the proffered water down, Melissa chanced a look at Brian. His eyebrows were like a dark slash over his blue eyes, his hair falling over his forehead, his one hand still holding his grandfather's shoulder, kneading it for comfort.

He looked forbidding but at the same time she couldn't help feeling a faint hitch in her heart at the concern he showed for his grandfather.

"What's wrong?" Brian asked, squatting down to get closer. "Why were you running?"

"Let me…get my…breath," Jack gasped, sucking in more air.

Melissa saw a flare of concern in Brian's eyes.

Then Jack took another drink and gave his grandson a weary look. "Someone broke into your garage."

"What? Are you okay?" Brian asked. "Why did you come running all the way here? Why didn't you phone? Why didn't you go to the police?"

"I'm fine. I didn't phone because I forgot your number and I didn't go to the police 'cause I thought you should know first." He waved off his grandson's flurry of agitated questions as he caught his breath. "I wouldn't have noticed but I went down to the garage to get a screwdriver. I'm sorry, son, but it looks like someone emptied your toolbox. Took all your wrenches, sockets, screwdrivers and pliers. Took the power tools, too."

"What? The power tools?" Brian's expression grew tight. Hard. "How in the world could they have done that?"

Jack blew out another sigh, looking glum in the face of his grandson's anger.

"If I ever catch the person who did this…"

Brian let the sentence trail off as he clenched his fists.

Fear flickered through Melissa as she shot Brian a sideways glance. He looked furious enough to do serious damage.

"Did you hear anything?" Brian asked his grandfather. "Anything that could give me an idea of the slimy thief?"

Jack blew out another sigh. "Didn't hear a car or truck. Whoever did it made a bunch of trips on foot. Had come and gone all morning. I didn't even notice." Jack looked at Brian, apology written all over his face. "I'm so sorry, son. I'm sorry I didn't catch whoever did it."

"No. Grandpa, don't say that," Brian replied, the harsh note in his voice at odds with his soothing words. "I'm glad you didn't go out there. You might have gotten hurt. It wouldn't have been worth it."

"But they got all your tools," Jack said, catching Brian by the arm. "I know how much those cost you."

"Won't your insurance cover that?" Melissa asked.

"Not for the full value." He gave her a clipped response. "Maybe a quarter. I'm on the hook for the rest."

Brian pulled in another breath, clenching and unclenching his fists. "So I guess I'll have to let

Joe Sheridan know." He looked over at Melissa, his blue eyes like flint. "Okay if I go and file a stolen goods report at the police station, boss?"

Melissa blinked at the cutting tone in his voice. "Of course," she said. "You don't have to ask."

"I'm thinking I do," he said. "After all, I'm just an employee. Bottom of the barrel. The last person you would choose."

Melissa's heart flopped over in her chest.

Guess he had heard every word she said.

Chapter Six

"We won't be able to do anything right away. Sorry, Brian." Joe Sheridan made a quick note on the report Brian had filled out, slipped it into a new file folder and dropped it into an already overflowing file tray. He pushed his baseball cap back on his thinning hair as he got up from a wooden chair behind a desk piled high with files and assorted papers. A computer that looked almost antique stood to one side beside the bits and pieces of paper pinned to the bulletin board. Behind the desk obscured wanted posters had been hanging there as long as Brian could remember. "Ever since I had to let Liston go, I've been swamped and shorthanded."

Brian pressed his lips together, trying not to let his exasperation and fear show. "So you won't be able to investigate it at all?"

"I can maybe come in a couple of days,"

he said, then the radio clipped to his shoulder squawked out a request. Joe reached over, clicked it and muttered something back. Then he turned to Brian. "Sorry, got a B & E I have to deal with on top of a nuisance report I've been trying to get at."

"That's more important than my missing tools?"

Joe gave him a pained look. "Sorry. You'll have to get in line. Besides, I'm sure your grandfather walked all over the footprints and I won't be able to figure anything out from them even if I come right away."

"The longer you wait, the more messed up they'll be," Brian protested.

"I'll come when I can." Joe held the door of his office open for Brian to exit.

Their footsteps echoed against the beaten cement walls, making Brian feel even more depressed. "Heard you were working at the bakery," Joe said as he pushed open a set of glass doors leading into the reception area. "How's that working out for you?"

Brian shot him an annoyed glance, wondering if he was hassling him, but Joe's brown eyes stared back at him devoid of mockery.

He shrugged. "It's a paycheck."

"I imagine you miss working at the factory," Joe said, resting his hands on the heavy belt weighed down with his holstered gun, flashlight and the other paraphernalia of a police officer.

"I do, but I'd hoped the SOS Committee would have approved my mechanic shop."

This netted him another apologetic look from Joe. "Yeah. Sorry that didn't work out for you." Then Joe grinned. "But who knows. That Melissa Sweeney is one good-looking girl. Maybe you two can—"

"Forget that," Brian said, holding up a hand to stop Joe. "I've got nothing to give any girl."

"Don't sell yourself short," Joe said. "You've got more to offer than you realize."

Brian's mind flashed to Melissa, his boss, the very person he had nothing to offer. Then he shrugged off Joe's comment, said goodbye and walked over to where his grandfather sat paging through worn and dog-eared magazines.

Grandpa looked up as Brian came near and slowly got to his feet. "So? We casing out the scene of the crime?" His eyes lit up with eager expectation as he rubbed his hands.

"Nope. Joe has more important stuff to deal with. They're short-staffed." Brian blew out a sigh of frustration. "Which means I can't make an insurance claim for the few dollars I'll get until they do a police report."

And the hits kept coming.

He dragged his hands over his face and tried

not to let the circumstances of his life beat at him. He'd managed to do a couple of oil changes over the weekend and had booked an engine overhaul for next week. It was a lot of work to get the grease out of his fingers so they looked good for his bakery work, but he was thankful for the mechanic jobs and the extra income they had brought in.

And now? He couldn't even do that.

"Thank goodness you have a job at the bakery," his grandfather said as they left the police station.

His grandfather meant well, but his comment made Brian even more frustrated.

If he hadn't been working at the bakery he might have been working in his shop. His garage wouldn't have been broken into because he would have been there. Now he would have to work for at least four months at the bakery just to get back to where he was financially when he started.

"I'll have to cancel that engine overhaul I was doing this week," Brian grumbled as they walked down Bronson Avenue to where his truck was parked. "I'll bring you home and then I should get back to work or I might lose that job, too."

Melissa's words still echoed in his head as they got to his truck. *Her last choice.*

He hated how her words had struck at the core of his being. It was hard enough to hear, period, but coming from her, a woman he couldn't help his attraction to, made it even harder to swallow.

"You want to have a look at the shop?" his grandfather asked when Brian dropped him off at the house on the outskirts of town.

"Actually I do." He turned his truck off. "I'll take a few pictures. Might help Joe solve this."

He pulled out his phone and he and his grandfather walked down the driveway to the shop.

"Guess I should have locked the shop," Brian said as he and his grandfather opened the door. "I never had to before."

"What is this town coming to?" His grandfather sighed. "Didn't think I'd see the day there would be a crime wave in our hometown."

Brian turned to his workbench, his heart dropping at the sight of the empty spaces where his grinder, cutoff saw, impact wrenches and compressor used to be. But what really tore at his soul was the open drawers of his mechanic tool chest. Empty. Hundreds of dollars worth of tools. Gone.

He thought of the new posters he had put up around town and in Concordia in the hope that he could drum up some more mechanic business.

And now?

Brian plunged his hand through his hair, frustration clawing at him. Now? Can that idea.

"Do you have any idea who could have done this?" Grandpa asked, his voice quiet, fully understanding how devastating this blow was to his grandson.

"Whoever did this wasn't wearing boots. Just running shoes and not big ones at that." Brian glanced down at the footprints again and shook his head as he snapped a few photos, then dropped his phone in his pocket.

Grandpa put his hand on Brian's shoulder. "I'll be praying for you, son. Praying that things will come together for you one way or the other."

Brian gave his grandfather a wry smile. "You better start off with praying my boss doesn't fire me. I really need this job now."

"Here's your scones, Miss Ann. Enjoy." Melissa forced a smile even as she felt as if her head would burst with each pound of her heart.

"Are you sure you should be working?" Ann Mars said as she took the crinkly paper bag from Melissa's hand. "You look all pale and shaky."

"It's what I do," she said as Ann nodded, then slowly shuffled out the door.

She had no choice but to work, Melissa

thought as she headed to the back of the bakery to frost the third layer of the anniversary cake she'd been trying to finish all afternoon. Amanda had a dentist appointment she had forgotten about and Brian had still not returned.

Twenty minutes and six customers later she was finally done piping the last of the pink and blue flowers. The cake was to be a replica of the couple's wedding cake, three tiers with the names swirled in icing on the top tier.

The back door opened and she looked up as Brian came into the bakery. As usual, he seemed to fill the space with his presence and as usual, Melissa's heart gave a tiny jump when she saw him.

She shook off her reaction, blaming her weakness on the headache that she couldn't shake.

"Did you figure anything out?" she asked, not encouraged by the scowl that darkened his handsome features.

Brian only yanked his apron over his head. "I spent way too much time filling out a police report that won't be looked at until tomorrow."

"I'm sorry," she said, not sure what else to say.

"Guess this is God's way of telling me what I should be doing."

"I'm not so sure God wanted your tools stolen," Melissa replied.

Brian arched one eyebrow her way, as if surprised by her comment. "I'm not so sure He wanted me to work here either, but here I am. Bottom of the barrel."

His words gave her a guilty start and she paused, giving him an apologetic look. "I didn't mean it the way it sounded."

"Really? How did you mean for it to sound?"

"I had to work off a list the SOS Committee gave me."

"And I was the last person on the list. So, bottom of the barrel," he huffed, walking past her to deal with a customer.

Melissa watched him go, annoyed with herself, knowing she shouldn't have said what she did.

Melissa leaned against the bench and closed her eyes. She could blame her previous outburst when she was talking to Dale on all kinds of things: Brian's ongoing resentment, the headache that dogged her.

Or the fact that, in spite of being exactly where she wanted to be doing exactly what she wanted to do, she still had a sense of something missing.

She glanced at Brian's retreating back, her heart giving the same little thump every time she saw him.

She turned back to the half-full bowl of frosting left over from the cake, trying to shake off the feeling. He had made it clear in many ways that he wasn't interested. In her or her bakery.

She wasn't feeling well. That was what her problem was. She'd been going full tilt since she came here, determined to prove herself to the community and the committee. All she needed was a good night's sleep. Things would look different tomorrow.

Maybe tomorrow Brian would forget what she had said.

That was the last of the customers. Brian locked the door of the bakery precisely at 5:30 and pulled the blinds on the bay windows.

He glanced at the display cases, disappointed to see how much product was left. He'd have to inventory the leftovers, package them as day-old and inform Melissa that today wasn't as good a day as yesterday.

And wasn't that an understatement! Bad day for Melissa, bad day for him. He was still fuming about the loss of his tools and Joe's inability to do anything about it.

But what bothered him even more was Melissa's easy dismissal of him.

Bottom of the barrel. He wondered why he cared what she thought. Wondered why he bothered to even let it concern him.

But it did. She was the first woman he'd been attracted to since Tracy. The first woman he was even remotely interested in.

He heard bread pans clanking around the back of the bakery. Melissa had been experimenting with a banana loaf recipe and judging from the occasional mutter it wasn't working out.

He felt like he should help but knew it wouldn't be welcomed. Since he started working for her, he had discovered that Miss Melissa was a perfectionist when it came to her baking. Amanda had been complaining to him the other day that Melissa only got her to do the most basic work.

So he kept his distance, her comment of this afternoon still stinging his pride.

He finished cleaning up the front and packaging the leftovers and then walked to the back of the bakery to clean there.

Melissa was bent over the large butcher-block workbench that took up most of the space in this part of the bakery, her elbows resting on the top. She was frowning at a piece of paper in front of her. She jumped when he set the trays of wrapped baked goods on the table, her frown deepening as she looked it over. "What am I going to do about all this?"

"Make less tomorrow, I guess," he replied

curtly. He was tired, too, and not feeling exactly charitable, but when he realized how he sounded, he tempered his reply with a smile.

But she turned away before she saw it.

"I'll put these in the refrigerator," he said.

She just nodded, her back still to him.

He set the trays on the large racks in the refrigerator and glanced at the top of the cake Melissa had just finished. Then he frowned when he saw what was written on the top.

"Do you know you got the wrong names on the cake?" he called out to Melissa.

"What?"

Brian picked up the top tier of the cake and brought it to her just as she came toward the cooler. "You made this for Peter and Ginny, right?"

Melissa nodded, staring down at the cake Brian still held.

"You misspelled Ginny. It's with a *G* not a *J* and it has two *N*s, not one."

Melissa blinked as she groaned in dismay. "Guess I'll have to fix that."

Brian moved toward the table to set it down for her.

"I can do that," she said, reaching for the cake. "I've got it."

"Your sleeve is dragging through the icing," she said, trying to shift the position of the cake.

"You have to fix it, anyway."

"Let me do it. Please." She gave another tug. He lost his grip just as he was about to set the cake on the counter. Melissa tugged again as if to counter his resistance and as a result pulled too hard.

Brian watched in horror as the cake, as if in slow motion, slid out of his hands and hovered a moment as Melissa attempted to compensate for her poor grip on the cardboard. The cake teetered, then dropped with a sickening plop onto the floor. Icing flew off to the side and the cake split into five pieces, each sliding in different directions off the cardboard onto the cement floor.

Silence followed the descent of the cake, then Melissa dropped to the floor beside it.

Brian also knelt down, though he could see there was nothing else to do but clean up the disastrous mess and start all over.

"Look what you did," Melissa cried, looking across at Brian, her eyes rimmed with red. Was she crying?

"I don't have time for this," she wailed.

"If you would have just let me put the cake down—"

"You should have given it to me—"

"I had it under control," Brian snapped, his own frustration with her, with the day, with his life spilling out in a rush of anger. "But you can't let anyone else have control, can you? You have to do it all yourself."

Melissa stared at him. With her eyes like two gimlets on him she reached down and grabbed some cake.

She looked at him, then at the cake and Brian could almost hear the gears grinding in her head.

She wouldn't.

Then she tossed it.

The gooey mess hit him square on his forehead and slid down the side of his face.

She did.

He blinked as what just happened registered. Then anger and frustration surged through him and before he could think he snatched up some of the cake and tossed it back at her. He didn't mean to hit her, but his aim, never good, was off and he got her on the side of her face.

She scowled at him and tossed another handful back. Just as quickly he returned the favor, his anger burning white hot by now.

Melissa reached down to the cake, still glaring at him. Pink, blue and white icing stuck in her hair, and cake and custard pudding clung to her face as she lobbed another piece at him that landed square on his nose.

Then her lip quivered, her shoulders shook and, to his surprise, she giggled, then chuckled.

Still holding his own handful of cake he watched in amazement as she leaned back against the legs of the counter, her hands clutched to her midsection as she dissolved into laughter.

She pointed at him. "You should see—" she gasped "—your face. Icing—" But she couldn't finish her sentence as cake and icing mixed with tears ran in a river of pink and blue down her cheeks.

A piece of cake slid down her face as she dropped her head back against the table, clutched her sides and shook with laughter.

Then Brian gave into the moment, releasing first a chortle, then a snicker and finally he, too, was bent over in the wreckage of the cake, waves of laughter rolling over him.

He chanced a look at her and the mess of icing and cake decorating her face, then he started again. He backhanded tears of laughter from his eyes, unable to say anything.

A piece of cake perched on the top of her head, threatening to slide down into her eyes, and he reached over and brushed it away. Then, pulling the cuff of his shirtsleeve down, he gently wiped a blob of icing from her forehead, then one from her cheek.

Her laughter died down as her eyes held his. He couldn't look away and didn't want to.

Another chuckle escaped her lips, then she eased out a happy sigh as, to his surprise, she reached over and wiped some cake from his face, too. Then she released a gentle smile. A genuine smile.

"I'm sorry." That was all she said.

Brian heard the sincerity in her voice and returned her smile, still holding her steady gaze. "I'm sorry, too."

He pushed the remnants of the now-destroyed cake aside and scootched over to sit beside her, too weak from laughter to sit on his own.

He took a deep breath and then another, rolling his head to look at her. Icing frosted her long eyelashes and shone on her face. Chunks of cake clung to her hair.

Trouble was she still looked beautiful.

"I meant it," she said, her voice quiet, still looking at him. "Today wasn't a good day for either of us. I'm sorry about your tools and I'm sorry about what I said about you being my last choice. I didn't mean…" She stopped herself there with a slow lift of her shoulders. Through the glistening frosting and the crumbs of cake he saw a flush stain her cheeks. "What I said came out wrong. I could blame it on this horrible headache and the way I'm feeling, but that's a cheat. I want to tell you how much I appreciate your hard work. I know this job wasn't your first choice and I feel bad that you've had to take it and I'm sorry I made you wear a pink-and-white-striped apron…

He was quiet a moment as her apology faded off into a sigh.

"Anyway, I'm sorry," she said. "I'm also truly sorry about your tools. I'm sure I would be as upset if someone took my knives or my mixer."

"Or your bread pans," he said.

Melissa laughed again, an easy tinkling laugh that shifted his equilibrium. "Is your grandfather okay?"

"Yeah. He's fine." He shot her a grateful smile. "Thanks for asking."

"He looked so overcome when he came to the park." Melissa stopped there, pressing her lips together as if remembering what she had said. Then she sighed. "And I'm so sorry you had to hear what I said to Dale. I wasn't thinking straight." She blew out a sharp breath. "I wasn't thinking at all. Please, believe me when I say you're not the bottom of the barrel."

"It would have to be a big barrel," Brian said.

Melissa chuckled, then grew serious. "You're

a good worker and you've taken a bad thing and made it work."

Her profuse apologies, admission and praise warmed the part of his heart that had been cool to her.

"I haven't been very gracious about it," he admitted.

"No, you haven't."

"It's just...working in a bakery was never part of my life's plan."

She eased out a wry smile. "It was always part of mine," she said quietly.

"Always?"

She shrugged. "When I was growing up I loved to bake."

"Where was growing up for you?"

Melissa pressed her hand against her forehead, her finger slipping over the icing on her hair. "All over. Gatlinburg for a while, Knoxville, Asheville, Grand Rapids, Rapid City... wherever my mother decided we needed to stay awhile."

"So you moved around a lot," he said, his voice quiet. He heard the faintest note of bitterness in her tone and wondered what her childhood had been like.

She shot him a quick sideways look. "Understatement." Then she lifted her apron and wiped icing from her face. He felt some slipping down his own face and was about to get it when she reached over and wiped his eyebrow. Her hand lingered a moment and a shiver teased his spine. He tamped his reaction as quickly as it came.

Sure, she was good-looking and appealing and pretty and interesting in spite of being a control freak.

But he had nothing to offer her. He couldn't support her. She was his boss; he was her employee.

Even as he reminded himself of his situation he couldn't stop the lift of his heart as their gazes held.

"Better get this cake cleaned up," he said, his voice suddenly gruff.

"I suppose," Melissa returned, dismay etched on her features. "And I suppose I'll have to make a new one now."

Brian got up and without thinking reached over to Melissa, catching her hand and pulling her to her feet.

For a moment they stood face to face, then Melissa laughed. "You need to wash up before you leave here," she said.

"So do you." He brushed another piece of cake from her face and again her smile faded as her expression grew serious. He wasn't sure if he had imagined the awareness radiating between them. Wasn't sure if it was simply the moment, or his lonely heart, or the realization that Melissa grew more appealing every day.

Chapter Seven

Watery light from the moon shone down on the back door of the bakery as Melissa pulled her keys out of her purse. As always, she glanced around the quiet back street, but all she saw was her shadow and the only sound was a rustling of leaves.

Who would be skulking around Bygones at five in the morning anyhow?

You, she thought.

She closed her eyes a moment as a flash of pain sliced through her skull. She should be home in bed, but that wasn't a luxury afforded to her. She had bread to bake.

Not as much as yesterday.

The thought taunted her and as she let herself into the bakery she indulged in a few seconds of self-pity, thinking of all the leftovers from the day before. Were the rumors going around town right? Was this bakery just a one-off? Were people already tired of her offerings? Were they truly unable to pay what she was charging?

She dropped her keys back into her purse and went into the tiny office off the front room. She looked at the recipes hanging on the wall: recipes for the cakes and tarts she was baking for Gracie Wilson's wedding.

It would be okay, she reminded herself. It would be okay.

She rummaged through her purse for the pain medication she had stocked up on yesterday. She shook a couple of pills out into her palm, then tossed them into her mouth.

Then almost choked on them.

A figure loomed in the back of the bakery. Tall. Broad shouldered. A really big person.

Her heart dove and her stomach flopped as her hand scrabbled for the rolling pin on the counter.

"Who's there?" she said, wishing her voice didn't sound so shaky as she grasped the handle.

"It's me." Really Big Person stepped into the single light Melissa had turned on and relief made her legs rubbery. "Brian."

"Were you really going to use that thing?" he asked as he took a few steps closer, his grin a white slash against his features.

Melissa looked from the rolling pin to him

then laid it on the table. "I would have if you were a bad guy. What are you doing here?"

Brian reached for his apron hanging on the hook beside Melissa's. "I've come to help you."

She frowned, glancing at the clock above the sink.

"Yeah. I'm early today. Eager to get going," he said, a surprising note of humor in his voice. He tied the strings of his apron, then walked over to her. "You don't look much better than you did yesterday."

"I'm feeling fine. You don't need to worry—" But her sentence was cut off as another flash of pain hit her. She gasped, pressing her fingers to her temple, and when she straightened Brian was studying her.

"Yeah. Real fine," he said dryly. "You should be home."

"I can't," she grumbled. "Who else could I get to do this?"

"Me."

She stared at him. "You?"

"Yeah. What's so bad about that?"

"Nothing. I guess. If I knew you were able to do this."

"I'm not incapable," he retorted.

Melissa was about to protest again when another burst of pain made her wince.

"Right," he said, striding past her, picking

up a plastic chair and bringing to her. "You sit yourself here and tell me what to do. That shouldn't be hard for you."

"I'm not that bossy," she declared as he set his hands on her shoulder and gently pushed down.

"I rest my case."

"I'll need to finish that cake," she said, her mind ticking back to the disaster of yesterday. In spite of the headache pounding through her head, she couldn't stop a smile thinking of how he looked after their cake fight.

"Cake after bread," he said. "I'm guessing we need flour and lots of it."

"I don't need to tell you where that is." She leaned back in the chair, waiting for the medication to kick in.

Brian saluted, then strode to the back of the bakery, whistling a tuneless ditty.

A few minutes later the first batch of dough was whirling around in the huge mixer, under her supervision, the dough winding around the hook, the hum of the machine a comforting sound.

"How long does that need to mix?" Brian asked as he washed his hands.

"A few minutes more and then you can proof it."

"Prove what?" Brian frowned as he hung up the hand towel.

"That the yeast works," she returned with a faint smile. Her head still felt as if someone was cutting through it with a dull knife, but she also felt as if a weight had fallen off her shoulders. Brian's presence created a surprising comfort.

She got up and ignored Brian's warning look as she slowly walked over to the other mixing bowl. "I'm just going to make up the cake," she told him when he frowned at her. "I'll take my time."

"Okay, but I'll do any heavy lifting required."

She gave a wan smile, hoping, praying she could get through the day intact. The pain was debilitating.

As the batter finished mixing and she was about to remove the bowl from the mixer, Brian nudged her aside. "Go grease the pan and I'll pour this in for you."

Ten minutes later the cake was in the oven and Brian was washing the bowl. "Now will you sit down?"

She was about to protest when Brian pointed at the chair, his expression brooking no discussion.

"I don't know if you realize how wrong this feels for me," she said, weakly giving in. "I'm usually here all by myself."

"And running the show single-handedly,"

Brian said, slanting her a teasing grin. "It's amazing what you get done in a day."

His unexpected praise warmed her heart.

"Not as much as I'd like to," she said. "Though I won't need to make as much today."

Brian set the clean bowl on the machine, then glanced over his shoulder. "The other day, when Eversleigh was asking you about bringing in business from other places, you said it was hard because you didn't have contacts in the area."

"I don't. I'm just a city slicker, after all."

To her surprise a flush tinted Brian's ruddy cheeks. "Yeah. Well, I'm sorry about that."

"It's true," she said. "I am a city slicker and I know local people were turned down to give me and Lily and the others an opportunity. I feel bad about it, but I wasn't letting the opportunity go by because of that."

"Nor should you have. But, like you said, it means you don't know the area. I do. And my friend Kirk's wife, Abby, she's in charge of the Farmer's Markets Association in Concordia and Junction City. I called her last night and asked her if there would be any room for you to sell some goods from the bakery. She was all excited and figured it would be a fantastic idea. She thinks people would be all over it."

His casual words created a swirl of varied emotions: surprise that he had thought of potential income for the bakery and, behind that, shock that Miss Coraline and Dale Eversleigh were right about Brian.

And she was wrong.

"Do you think I could sell enough?" she asked, practicality tamping down the possibilities.

Brian shrugged. "Abby seemed to think so."

Melissa bit her lip, her mind suddenly churning. "How would this work? How would we find the time for doing all that?"

"The farmer's markets run on Saturdays. We could do Concordia one week and see how it goes. We could bake enough on Friday so you don't have to on Saturday. Let Amanda run the store on Saturday. If it works out, after Gracie Wilson's wedding is out of the way, we could look at doing it every week."

We could, he had said. "Do you figure on coming along?" she blurted out.

"I could, if you want me to," he said as the timer dinged. "So now what?"

She instructed Brian how to cut the dough into pieces and drop them into the kneading machine. When the dough was done, he mixed up another batch while Melissa got the baking pans ready. Brian protested, but she told him she was feeling better.

Which she was. Having Brian helping made

her feel as if she could, at least for today, lay down a burden she'd hauled around since starting this bakery. She had been on her own, doing it all, carrying it all since she came to Bygones and even before. Having him around this morning was probably a one-off, but for today, it was good. Today, in spite of the misgivings dogging her every time she got close to a man, today his presence made her soul feel blessed.

"So do you really think that could work?" Melissa asked as she dropped the kneaded rolls of bread into the baking pans. "The farmer's market thing?"

"It's worth a try," Brian said, dumping another huge container of flour into the mixer. "You obviously can make more than the local townspeople can buy. It would definitely get your name out into the other towns."

"So what would we sell there?" Melissa asked, getting the next pans ready, her hand working automatically as the bread dough dropped into the kneader, was flattened, then rolled into bread loaves.

As they talked, the tension shadowing her and Brian's relationship seemed to have eased away with the icing and cake that had been liberally spread over the bakery yesterday.

They discussed some of the items Brian thought would sell and what Melissa thought would be easy to make as they moved from making bread to buns. With each plan Melissa grew more hopeful about the future of the bakery.

"Are we done for now?" Brian asked as he wheeled the last rack of bread pans into the large metal-lined room that held a small heater to help the bread rise.

Melissa glanced at the clock, surprised to see how early it still was. "The first batch doesn't need to go in for half an hour."

"Great. Let's write down some of the things we talked about," Brian said.

His involvement surprised her. She was tempted to ask him why this mattered now when he'd been such a reluctant employee before, but then she thought of something Miss Coraline had told her.

Get Brian involved in the decision-making process and maybe he would be more invested in the bakery's success.

They walked together to her little office, and as she sat down, Brian came in behind her. Once again she was aware of how tall he was, how broad his shoulders. How he filled up the space. And as they made their plans, it was if her senses were heightened around him, creating another kind of tension. He was so…vitally present in her office. It thrilled her a little and scared her a little.

"So how are you feeling now?" Brian asked after they finished the list, leaning back against the desk behind him, his arms folded over his chest.

"Not as sick as a few hours ago."

"You still look washed out," he said. "You sure you don't want to go home for a bit? Lie down?"

Again, his concern created a shift in the atmosphere. She looked up and their gazes locked.

A hint of a smile edged his well-shaped lips, softening his strong features. Then he reached out and touched her face. His rough fingers slid over her skin, igniting a flicker of anticipation. Then he plucked something out of her hair and held it out for her inspection.

A bit of cake.

"You must have been tired last night," he said, wiping it off on his apron as he grinned at her.

"I was," she admitted with a light laugh, checking her hair in case she had missed something else. "Still am."

"I'm not surprised. You put in long days." He tilted his head to one side as if studying her. "Did you know it would be like this?" he asked. "This much work?"

Melissa pondered that question, then shook

her head. "I knew it would be hard, but I never realized how much responsibility it would be. I guess that's part of running your own business." She held his steady gaze. "Did you know what you wanted to get into? When you were thinking of starting up your own mechanic business?"

Brian shrugged. "I had a good idea. I had been doing mechanic work in the evenings and weekends for a couple of years before I applied for a loan. But I guess God has another plan now that my tools are gone," he said.

She frowned at him. "I didn't think someone as big and tough looking as you would be the type that depended on God."

"I've depended on God in every part of my life," he said, speaking quietly but with conviction. "From when I was a kid I was told this world belongs to God and that I am to use what I've been given to serve Him and love Him. It was how my parents and grandparents raised me and my sisters."

Melissa felt a flicker of envy at his sincerity. "That's remarkable and comforting," she said. "To have that legacy of faith."

"I take it your family didn't?"

"I was raised by a single mother who taught me that the only person to take care of me was me. God or Jesus didn't figure much in my mother's life."

Brian released a light laugh. "Taking care of yourself is good in theory, but I think we're people made for relationships. We exist in a web of them—family, community, God."

"Are your parents part of that web?"

Brian's smile faded. "They were. They died… a few years ago." The words were ragged and harsh and sorrow unfurled in Melissa's heart.

"I'm so sorry to hear that. I didn't know."

"How could you?" he said quietly. "You're still new here."

At one time him saying that might have made her feel defensive, but she realized it was her reality. "I'm still sorry. That must have been hard for you."

"I'm thankful God gave me and my sisters strength to deal with it. My grandfather reminds me regularly that control is an illusion."

His words teased out an old memory of a minister preaching about letting go of control of one's life. The words had seemed ironic to Melissa because then she had had so little control and her mother had so much. They moved around from place to place on her mother's whims. Melissa had learned early on that she had to take care of herself.

But in spite of her constant reminder to stay

independent, the memory of what that minister said grew, whispering around the edges of her mind and holding a promise of peace and rest. She blinked, but the feeling didn't dissipate. In fact, as she held Brian's sincere gaze it grew and called louder.

"You're blessed to have a grandfather," Melissa said, trying to ignore the words that created such a yearning in her. "I'm jealous of that. I never knew my father and my mother was an only child."

"Did you know any of your family?"

"I remember my grandmother. We lived with her for about six months. She took me to church."

"Did you enjoy it? Church?"

His question created a thrum of melancholy as the thoughts she had struggled to dampen now assaulted her. She was reminded of a relationship with God tentatively begun as a teenager. "I did."

"Would you go again?"

Melissa weighed that thought. "I don't imagine God wants someone who spent some time with Him when it was convenient and then ignored Him when it wasn't."

Brian chuckled and again Melissa was surprised at her reaction to his genuine smile. "God's shoulders are broad. I think He'd be pleased if you spent time with Him again, like any parent would. Going to church would be a good start."

Melissa held that thought close as it ignited a surprising warmth in her. "I'd like to think about it. Maybe." It was all she could give him.

Then the timer went off and Brian pushed himself away from the desk to get to the next job. Melissa moved to get up but a wave of dizziness washed over her.

"You stay right here." Brian laid his hands on her shoulders and gently pushed her down. "I'll take care of the bread."

"You need to know how to space the loaves in the oven. They have to be put in properly so they brown evenly." Melissa tried to get up again.

"Okay. You can tell me that, but you're doing it sitting down. In that white chair I got for you," Brian said firmly. Then, to her utter amazement, he helped her up, slipped her arm in his and walked with her to the other chair. As he sat her down, her hair slipped over her face. He reached up and tucked it behind her ear. Then he gave her a careful smile.

As their eyes held something stirred in her chest—the beginnings of affection for this man and his surprising solicitude.

Did she dare?

The only person to take care of you is you.

Her mother's voice, her constant companion as Melissa had navigated the pain of Jason breaking up with her and abandoning her, returned, reminding her to be careful.

But being the only person to take care of me is exhausting, Melissa thought as she watched Brian wheel the cart holding the risen bread to the oven, then place the bread on the revolving racks inside.

Sometimes she wanted to have someone she could depend on. Someone stronger than her who could hold her up.

She just wasn't sure who that person could be.

Then Brian shot her a smile and again she felt a surprising connection so ethereal and vague she wasn't sure she could pinpoint what it was or how it began.

All she knew for certain was that it gave her some curious comfort she wasn't sure what to do with. Wasn't sure she dared embrace. Opening herself up to that connection meant letting someone else in her life. It meant letting someone else determine the course of her life.

Did she dare do that again?

Chapter Eight

"I thought we could set up the food buffet with the buns and coffee here," Mrs. Morgan said, waving an imperious hand toward the west wall of the basement of the church. She came to an abrupt halt in the middle of the room, a frown creasing her forehead as she looked up at the ceiling. "Though we need to do something about those horrible exposed pipes."

Not my department, Melissa thought, keeping her eyes rigidly focused on the piece of paper with the list of items Mrs. Morgan had requested for the buffet.

Yesterday, after Amanda came to work, Brian had insisted Melissa go back to her apartment and get some rest. She did, and to her surprise, she had fallen asleep as soon as she dropped onto her bed. A few hours later when she returned to the bakery she announced to Brian and Amanda that she felt much better and told Brian she didn't need his help the next morning. She had felt the beginnings of emotions that scared her. It was better that she and Brian keep their distance.

However, this morning Brian was waiting at the back door of the bakery, leaning against the wall, his arms crossed over his chest, sleeves rolled up in spite of the cool morning air. He was whistling the same song he'd been whistling yesterday.

Melissa went through the motions of protesting his help, but Brian ignored her. She did feel better this morning and having Brian around had, once again, created curious feelings.

He hadn't even protested much when Melissa gave him a list of things she wanted him to do at the bakery this morning so she could make this meeting with Mrs. Morgan and Josh.

"Melissa, are you making note of this?" Mrs. Morgan asked.

As Melissa glanced Mrs. Morgan's way, she heard a muffled chuckle and didn't dare look over at Josh, who stood beside her, his hands in his pockets and obviously not taking note of the problem of the exposed pipes either.

"No matter—maybe we can dress them up with tulle," Mrs. Morgan said. "What do you think, Gracie?"

Melissa looked up in time to see Gracie shoot Melissa a pleading glance. Then Melissa heard the click and the creak of a door opening upstairs.

"I think I hear Lily," Melissa said, granting Gracie a momentary reprieve. "I know she wanted to go over placement of the flower arrangements with you, Gracie."

Gracie shot Melissa a thankful look, then fled upstairs. But the solution was only momentary as Mrs. Morgan turned to Josh and Melissa, raising one finger. "Excuse me a moment. I should talk to Lily, too." Then she swept out of the basement and up the stairs.

Melissa stifled a sigh, scribbled a few notes on her clipboard and glanced over at Josh, who was watching Mrs. Morgan go, an enigmatic look on his face.

"So what did you think of the meeting Tuesday night?" Melissa asked.

Josh turned his attention back to her, then granted her a crooked smile. "I thought it went well. Miss Coraline is certainly a cheerleader for the town. Have you come up with any ideas since then?"

"Yesterday morning Brian suggested I consider taking baked goods to the farmer's market in Concordia next Saturday and, possibly, Junction City a couple of weeks later."

Josh nodded, stroking his chin with his long fingers, as if thinking. "I'm surprised."

"You don't think it's a good idea?"

"I think it's a great idea. I'm surprised he's making suggestions considering how negative he was about your business at the grand opening last month."

Melissa couldn't help a faint frisson of concern. She agreed that Brian's change was a bit abrupt, but at the same time she felt that things had changed between them in other, uncertain ways. She wasn't sure what to think of it all—only that she was seeing a side of Brian that appealed to her.

"He's been helping me with the baking."

Josh's eyebrows shot up into his dark hair. "Really? I wonder what made him change that much."

Melissa tried not to blush as her mind ticked back to the cake fight. She knew she could pinpoint the change in him at that moment.

And the change in her.

Then Josh grinned. "Okay. I think I know what's going on."

"Nothing's going on." The flush warming her cheeks belied her protest. "Never mind," she said, about to leave, her own emotions growing increasingly unsure when Josh caught her lightly by the arm.

"Sorry. I won't tease you anymore. Don't go yet. I was hoping I would have a chance to talk some business with you."

Melissa stopped and simply nodded, still feeling self-conscious about her reaction to Josh's teasing.

"When Coraline was talking about initiatives for growing the business I thought of something. What would you say if you supplied my coffee shop with your sausage rolls, croissants, Danish pastries and some loaf cakes and gave me an exclusive on those items?"

"What do you mean?"

"You would sell them to me and I could offer them to my customers along with their coffee. It would give you another outlet for your baked goods and give me value-added service for my shop." He held up a finger. "But, like I said, I would get an exclusive, so if someone wants, let's say, a cranberry scone, they can only get them at my coffee shop—not at my coffee shop and your bakery."

Melissa thought about this a moment, then nodded. "I think that could work."

"Great. I need to boost business and I know many people buy food at your bakery and come to my coffee shop to eat it." Josh spread his arms out. "I would be doing them a community service and saving them a few steps."

"Why don't you come over to the bakery next week and we can put together a list of items you could carry?"

"Great. Thanks a bunch for this, Melissa. You really helped me out."

"Hey, us newcomers have to stick together," Melissa said.

"Yeah. I hear ya. Every day I get the gears from yet another old-timer who can't believe what I charge for a cup of coffee."

"I get the same thing about my tarts and cakes."

"Guess it will take time." Josh grinned and was about to say more when they heard the clatter of footsteps on the stairs. Gracie flew around the corner, her head down and her hand covering her face.

"Gracie. Are you okay?" Melissa hurried to her side, shocked to see tears on the young girl's cheeks.

Gracie blinked, then dashed the back of her hand across her eyes. "Sorry. I'm just…I don't know…it's too much…I don't think…"

"You're just suffering from pre-wedding jitters," Melissa assured her. "It'll be okay."

"Will it?" Gracie asked, then shot an anguished look behind her as Mrs. Morgan called out Gracie's name.

Gracie caught Melissa by the arm. "Tell her I

got sick," she said, then flew out the other door and up the back stairs.

Mrs. Morgan appeared as the door on the opposite side of the room fell shut behind Gracie. She looked around, her lips pinched together. "Where is that girl? We're not done here."

"She asked me to tell you she got sick," Melissa said. "Sorry."

Mrs. Morgan heaved out a sigh, then with a shake of her head went back up the stairs again.

"I should go talk to Gracie," Melissa said, turning to Josh. "Tomorrow I'll be at the farmer's market, so stop by the bakery on Monday and we can talk more about your proposal."

She went out the same door Gracie had flown out of but when she stepped outside, all she saw was the back of Gracie's car heading down the street.

Nothing to do here, she thought and turned back to the building to see if Lily needed any help. But when she entered the sanctuary of the church, Lily was gone.

Melissa paused a moment in the cool quiet of the church.

Muted light from the simple stained-glass windows ran across the top of the sanctuary, spilling in colored beams onto the wooden pews. The front of the church had an arched opening framing a rough wooden cross. The pulpit stood to one side, a wooden box with a lectern and microphone. A banner with an image of a loaf of bread held by weathered hands graced one wall. The words below the image proclaimed, *"I am the Bread of Life."*

Appropriate, she thought, looking back to the cross at the front of the church, remembering the small one that had hung in the church she had gone to all those years ago.

As she stood, she heard a still, small voice calling her, inviting her to sit.

So she did, slipping into the last pew, resting her hands on the top of the bench in front of her. The silence of the building bid her to be still, be silent. To wait.

She drew in a deep breath, cleansing her mind and soul, then sat back. As she did she saw a Bible resting on the bench beside her and she picked it up.

It had been years since she had read the Bible. The pastor at the church her grandmother took her to had given her one. Melissa used to read it every night.

Then it got lost in one of the moves and was never replaced. Melissa had long suspected her mother had thrown it out. She had never supported Melissa's foray into faith, saying it was for weak people who couldn't make it on their own.

Melissa paged through this worn Bible, noting the markings on the pages, the well-thumbed corners. She stopped here and there to read a highlighted piece, wondering what it was about that particular passage that had spoken to the owner of this well-loved Bible. She stopped at one passage that was marked with a bookmark and started reading.

Then Jesus declared, "I am the bread of life. Whoever comes to me will never go hungry, and whoever believes in me will never be thirsty."

The same words as the banner in the front of the church. They settled into a familiar place in her soul, feeding a hunger she knew had been there ever since she had first gone to church with her grandmother.

"Can I help you?"

The sudden voice made her jump.

A tall, slim man stood behind her, the sunshine from the window behind him lighting up the fringe of light reddish-brown hair circling his head. Kind eyes glinted at her from beneath bushy eyebrows. A thick mustache framed his smiling mouth.

"I'm Hugh Garman, the pastor here. You're Melissa Sweeney, the lady who runs the bakery."

"Guilty as charged," Melissa said, still holding the Bible. "I thought I would come and look…just sit a moment… I know it's not Sunday. Sorry." She moved to get up when Pastor Garman held his hand out in a calming motion.

"Don't worry. We have had many people stopping in to pray for one thing or another the past few months. It's been a difficult time for our community."

"I understand that." Melissa thought of Brian being laid off from the factory and being forced to work in the bakery. She wondered what adjustments other people had had to make.

"I hope you do," Pastor Garman said. "I know we can't expect a sudden turnaround in our town's fortunes, but the fact that someone was willing to put money into your business gives us some hope."

Melissa felt it again. The steady burden she and her fellow new shopkeepers carried. The expectation that their businesses would make a difference. What it if wasn't enough?

"I hope what I'm doing helps," she said with a wry smile. Then she looked down at the book she still clutched in her hands and held it out to him. "I found this Bible."

Pastor Garman smiled. "That would be mine. I came back to get it."

"I was just reading the piece about how Jesus says He is the bread of life," Melissa said. "It kind of spoke to me."

"I guess, as a baker, it would," he said, his

deepening smile creating wrinkles around the corners of his friendly eyes. "It's the passage for my sermon this Sunday."

"The same as the one on the banner," Melissa said, waving her hand in the direction of the front of the church.

"That was the point."

She smiled.

"You're welcome to join us on Sunday," Pastor Garman said, taking the Bible and holding it close. "We're having a picnic afterward. The Dills are providing pizza and snacks. The picnic would be a good way to meet some other people in the community." He gave her a knowing smile. "Maybe ease some of the resistance people might have to your being here."

"I don't think boosting my business would be the right reason to come to church."

Pastor Garman's smile remained steady as his eyes held hers. "Then come for another reason. Come for the food."

Melissa was taken aback at his reply.

Pastor Garman gestured to the banner at the front of the church. "More than one way to be nourished this Sunday," he said.

Melissa couldn't help but smile at his double meaning. "I'll think about it."

Then, to her surprise, he reached over and pulled a Bible out of the pew and gave it to her.

"Why don't you start with this?" he said. "Look at it as preparation for your visit on Sunday if it makes you feel better."

Melissa took the Bible, touched at his consideration. She looked at the book, then back at him. "Thanks for this."

"Just promise to read it and to put your trust in God for your life, okay?"

Melissa nodded even as her inner voice warned her that trust was a precious commodity. She had trusted her parents to take care of her, and her father, until she was five, but they packed her all over the country. Her mother, after her father left, carried on in the same tradition.

And after Jason hurt her she had learned to be careful with her trust.

Brian swept the last of the crumbs from the floor around the bread slicer onto the dustpan and dumped them into the bin. Amanda was gone for the day and Melissa was washing up the last mixing bowl. It was only the two of them working in the quiet of the bakery, the only sounds the swish of water in the sink and the hum of the refrigerator. Tomorrow was Sunday and Brian was looking forward to a day off.

Brian had come again this morning to help

Melissa. This was the third time, and he was figuring out what to do. Though his head buzzed with weariness, working with Melissa all day held a curious appeal.

Although before he had been reluctant to work in the bakery, he had admired Melissa. Now that admiration was morphing into something deeper. Stronger. It scared him because, despite his changing feelings for her, nothing else in his life had changed. He was as far away from his goal as he ever had been.

He was still Melissa's employee, and the dream of being his own boss was a shimmering mirage.

"How are you feeling now?" he asked, concerned at the flush that still tinged her cheeks.

"I feel better. Thanks for asking."

"Hey, gotta take care of the boss," he said, her sincere smile doing interesting things to his heart.

As he tugged his apron off, he watched Melissa wipe down the counter. Then she turned to him and again it was as if awareness blossomed between them, heightening the moment, creating a surprising tension.

A knock on the back door broke into the moment. Brian poked his thumb over his shoulder.

"Sorry. My grandfather. He needed to use my truck today, so he's picking me up."

But before he could go to the back, the door opened and his grandfather came inside. His bright blue eyes darted over the bakery, then came to rest on Melissa.

"Well, hello again, Miss Sweeney. I trust your oven is working okay."

Brian inwardly cringed at the sight of his grandfather. Ever since Grandpa had seen Melissa, he'd been bugging Brian to have her over, reminding him that the poor girl was all alone in Bygones and could use the company.

"It's working fine," Melissa said, cutting a self-conscious look Brian's way as if remembering what she had said then.

"And how's Brian been working for you?" Grandpa continued.

"Grandpa, I think we should get going," Brian cut in. "Miss Sweeney is tired."

"Well, then I don't imagine you have much energy for making supper," he said, rubbing his thin hands together as if making plans.

Brian wanted to hustle his grandfather out of the bakery, sensing exactly where he was headed.

"I was going to get something from The Everything," Melissa said.

"That's crazy talk," Grandpa said with a quick frown. He poked a bony finger in Brian's chest. "Can't have that poor young girl heading home with some sloppy old pizza from the Dills, can we?"

"The Dills' pizza is pretty good," Brian said, shooting a warning frown his grandfather's way.

But Grandpa's tunnel vision was in full effect today and he looked back at Melissa. "Why don't you come and join us?" he said. "I've got pork tenderloin, fresh green beans from the community garden and spinach salad."

"I wouldn't want to impose on your time with your grandson," Melissa murmured.

Brian guessed she felt as awkward as he did.

"Nonsense," his grandfather blustered. "I get more than enough time with Brian. Too much time, in fact. It would be lovely to have the company of a pretty young woman at the house."

"You're starting to sound like Dale Eversleigh," Brian warned.

"That old bounder? Not a chance. I have more class than that," his grandfather protested, still not making eye contact with Brian. He walked over to Melissa's side and caught her by the arm. "You come. Join us. I'll feel insulted if you don't."

Brian sensed her hesitation and guessed it had more to do with spending time with him than it did with imposing on his time with his grandfather.

Then, to his surprise, she said, "Okay. I'd love to."

"That's excellent," Grandpa said, shooting Brian a triumphant look. "Isn't that excellent, grandson?"

Brian gave his grandfather a wan smile. He wasn't sure how excellent it was. He was certain that spending time with Melissa at his house would make it harder to be around her at the bakery.

His grandfather waved his hand toward the back door. "Follow us in your car. We won't lead you wrong."

Brian shot Melissa one more look, trying to gauge her reaction to his grandfather's goading.

Her mouth was curved in a light smile, as if the thought of eating supper with someone else was appealing to her.

Trouble was, it was appealing to him, too.

Too much so.

Chapter Nine

"I'm reading from a passage in Romans," Jack Montclair said, his white head bent over the Bible in front of him. He looked up at Melissa and smiled. "It's one of my favorite books in the Bible written by Paul, who, at one time, persecuted the church. The book of Romans lays out some of the great truths of faith and what God does for us."

"It's not Sunday, Grandpa," Brian said with a nervous laugh. "Melissa doesn't need a sermon."

"It's okay. I don't mind at all," Melissa said. "I'd like to find out more about what the Bible teaches."

She was surprised when, after the meal, Brian got up and, as if it was the most normal thing in the world, pulled a Bible out of a drawer and placed it on the table in front of his grandfather.

He had glanced her way, asking her if she minded. She shook her head, touched he had considered her feelings and, at the same time, admiring Brian's basic faith.

Brian held her gaze, then a gentle smile softened his strong features and she felt her heart quicken in response. For what seemed like the fiftieth time, she wondered what she had been thinking when she had accepted Jack's invitation to come for supper.

The appeal of spending more time with Brian in a place that wasn't the bakery had been a factor. But now that she was here, she felt self-conscious. Far too aware of the changing feelings between them, feelings she wasn't sure she dared indulge in.

"This is where we left off," Grandpa continued. He paused a moment, as if preparing himself. *"If you declare with your mouth, 'Jesus is Lord,' and believe in your heart that God raised him from the dead, you will be saved. For it is with your heart that you believe and are justified and it is with your mouth that you profess your faith and are saved."*

The words teased up a memory of her grandmother sitting beside her on the bed. They would read together from the Bible, quietly so Melissa's mother, who slept in the room next door, couldn't hear.

Melissa remembered the feeling of trust she felt, the feeling of being surrounded by love, when she told her grandmother that yes, she did believe this.

Those feelings of vulnerability returned now as she listened to Jack reading from his Bible. She needed faith. She couldn't live her life completely on her own. The thought was so opposite of what her mother taught her that she felt an automatic resistance.

But she had lived her life on her own the past few years and she hadn't liked it. She yearned for those moments she had shared with her grandmother. Yearned for the peace God could give her.

Jack finished reading, closed the Bible and prayed. And as he prayed, Melissa felt a sense of comfort and strength. A sense that she wasn't alone.

When Jack was done, she waited a moment, her head still bent, and blinked away unexpected moisture from her eyes.

"Are you okay?" Brian asked, reaching across the table and covering her hand with his.

She swallowed, her heart fluttering at the warmth and unexpectedness of his touch. Then she looked up at him and nodded. "Yeah. I'm fine."

His eyes locked on her as if trying to decipher

what she was saying, then he gently squeezed her hand and nodded. "That's good."

She held his earnest gaze and for a moment she also yearned for someone to be beside her. For a partner in her life. Someone she could lean on.

Brian?

She shook the feeling off. She had her plans in place and she couldn't let Brian distract her. The bakery was her focus and she had to remember that she was the only one who cared about it.

So she pulled her hand back and got to her feet.

"Now because I made supper, I get out of doing the dishes," Jack announced with glee as he also stood.

"Of course you do," Melissa said, giving him a quick smile. "I just want to tell you how much I appreciated eating a home-cooked meal. I seldom cook for myself."

"Really?"

"I'm baker, not a cook," Melissa said with a self-conscious smile as she started cleaning up.

"No. Stop," Brian protested, taking the plates from her as their fingers brushed. "You should go home. Get some rest."

"I'm not that tired," she said, pulling her hand back so quickly she almost dropped a plate. "I can surely help with the dishes. Pay for my supper that way."

Brian looked like he was about to protest again when Jack clapped him on the shoulder. "You don't want to argue with that one," he said with a twinkle in his eye. "Looks to me like she's the kind of woman who always gets her way." He winked at Melissa, then walked through the doorway into the living room beyond and dropped into a large easy chair.

Brian shrugged. "Suit yourself, but you need to know there's no dishwasher."

"Then I guess we'll have to wash the dishes by hand," she said, realizing what she'd gotten herself into.

Doing dishes with Brian.

Though they spent a lot of time at the bakery together, somehow, doing dishes in his kitchen created a different ambience than working in the bakery.

The bakery was her territory.

This was his, she thought as she stepped into the kitchen.

She looked around and a sense of home and comfort enveloped her like a gentle hug.

The cupboards flanking two walls were painted in chartreuse and had ceramic knobs in the shape of yellow flowers. The countertop was a soft caramel granite. A large window with a deep ledge holding a number of plants sat above the double sink, illuminating the room with soft evening light.

"What a charming kitchen," Melissa said, setting the plates by the sink. Then she noticed the stove built into a bricked-in alcove. Six burners. Gas. Stainless steel. Large oven.

A baker's dream.

"What a beautiful stove," she exclaimed, walking toward it, running her hand over the front of it and noticing an extra faucet built into the wall above the stove. How convenient.

"Kind of wasted on me," Brian said as he scraped the leftovers from the plates into the sink. "My appliance of choice is the microwave. Grandpa likes cooking, though, so he appreciates it."

Melissa turned, taking in the rest of the kitchen. Stainless steel refrigerator with two doors and beside it the frosted glass doors of a walk-in pantry. "This kitchen is amazing."

"My mother fixed this up five years ago," Brian explained. "Put in a garbage disposal and that fancy stove but no dishwasher. Her philosophy was that the best conversations happen while doing dishes together." He ran some water and turned on the disposal unit, then put in the stopper and filled the sink with steaming water. "Trouble is that's usually when me and my sisters fought the most."

"You had sisters?"

"Two. Holly and Louisa. Holly lives in Manhattan. Works for a mortgage broker. Louisa settled in Kansas City. They could hardly wait to shake the dust of Bygones off their feet."

"You get along with them?" Melissa asked, curious about the other part of Brian's life. "Do you see them much?"

"Yeah. They're great girls. This spring, after the factory closed, I went to Manhattan to visit Holly. She took me around to see the sights. Went to a play off-Broadway, saw the Empire State Building, the Statue of Liberty, Central Park, City Hall, a place called the Woolworth Building. We couldn't go inside, but we could look a the beautiful architecture."

"Wow. I've been many places but never to New York."

Brian shrugged as he put dishwashing liquid in the warm water. "It was good, but I was glad to be back here. Back home."

Home. Melissa wondered if she would ever feel that way about Bygones. She had never put roots down anywhere. Even in St. Louis she'd lived, as she did here, in a furnished apartment. She'd never even owned her own furniture.

"This is a good home," she said quietly, wondering where she would be after she fulfilled the two years required by the SOS Committee. Would she be making a home here? Alone?

Brian shot her a look over his shoulder, then smiled. "Yeah. It is. Hopefully someday things will be back to normal again."

"Normal?"

"The way it was…before," he said quietly.

Before she came, she thought. Is that what he meant? But she found she didn't want to ask. Her feelings were in flux lately and Brian was making her more confused. She didn't like feeling as if she wasn't in charge.

Brian turned on the water, rolled up his sleeves and dropped the dishes into the sink.

"Where's a towel?" Melissa asked, trying to sound crisp and businesslike. They might as well get this done. "I'll dry."

Brian tilted his chin in the direction of a drawer. She grabbed a towel and they worked in silence for a while, then Brian looked her way. "You seemed touched by what Grandpa read," he said.

Melissa concentrated on getting the moisture off the plate, trying not to let her emotions take over, but at the same time she knew he had seen her tears. "I was. I…I was reminded of a conversation I once had with my grandmother."

"What conversation was that?"

Why did he care?

But at the same time she felt as if it had been so long that she'd had a chance to talk to anyone about her faith, the words seemed to spill out, needing expression.

"I remember her asking me if I believed I needed Jesus in my life," she said.

Brian rested his hands on the edge of the sink, soap suds clinging to them, his head tilted to one side, his blue eyes probing into her soul. "And did you?"

She couldn't look away from his sincere gaze and sensed that her answer was important to him. Then she nodded. "I did then. I do now, too."

Brian's smile too easily eased past the barriers she had been trying to keep around her heart. Around her soul. "That's not easy to admit," he said quietly. "I still have to remind myself that I can't do it all on my own."

Melissa only nodded, his words a strong echo of her own struggles.

They worked in silence for a few more minutes. "So, did you hear about the church picnic on Sunday?" he asked.

Melissa nodded. "Pastor Garman told me about it."

"Are you going?"

"I think I should. As a business owner it would probably help."

She caught his frown and sensed this was not exactly the right thing to say, but she couldn't take it back now.

"When did you talk to Pastor Garman?"

"When I was at the church the other day, helping Gracie and Mrs. Morgan with the wedding."

"He's a good man."

"He invited me to church, too."

"Would you attend?"

Melissa tested the thought, her mind ticking back to how she felt when Brian's grandfather read the Bible. "I think I'd like to. Though Pastor Garman told me it would be good from a PR perspective, I'd like to think I'm going for another reason."

Brian's easy laugh did goofy things to her stomach. He seemed more relaxed, more comfortable with himself here.

More appealing.

Melissa placed the last cleaned and dried cup in the cabinet and set the damp towel on the counter, thankful she was done. Being around Brian in his house was different from being around him in the bakery. Different in a slightly scary way.

Different in a far too fascinating way.

"So I guess that's the last of the dishes," she

said, glancing around the cozy kitchen one more time as if checking.

Brian wiped his hands on the towel she had just laid down, then looked over at her.

Their gazes locked and the space between them seemed heavy with unspoken thoughts and emotions.

Part of her mind cried out a warning, but her lonely soul made her hold his gaze. Made her lean ever so slightly toward him, giving in to the push and pull that she had been struggling with ever since their cake fight.

Then, to her surprise and consternation, Brian reached out and touched her face.

His fingers were warm, gentle. Disturbing.

"Something on my cheek?" she said with a shaky laugh, surprised at her reaction to his simple touch. Surprised at how natural it seemed.

He shook his head. "No."

Her heart turned over at his quiet admission, and for a moment she had to stop her own hand from reaching out and touching him. Connecting with him.

She swallowed and looked away, confusion warring with the attraction she knew was growing between them.

Did she dare? Could she do this?

Would he let her down as the other men in her life had?

* * *

"May the Lord bless you and keep you. May He make His face shine upon you and give you peace."

Brian drew in a long, slow breath. Peace. It had been a long time since he had felt peace in his soul.

Having the factory close and struggling to make ends meet. He closed his eyes, letting Pastor Garman's words settle into his soul and nourish him. He needed to let go of his expectations—he knew that.

Then he glanced at Melissa standing beside him. When they had met this morning at the back of the church his Grandpa, who Brian suspected was trying to get them together, had invited her to come and sit with them. To his surprise, she accepted.

And the whole worship service he had struggled with his feelings toward her. He was attracted to her. Who wouldn't be? But he knew things were shifting and changing between them. He had been attracted to women before, but something about Melissa—her independence, her work ethic, her honest struggle with her faith—all came together to create an appeal he had never felt for any other woman before.

At the same time, her independence generated a curious ambivalence. On the one hand, he admired it, but on the other, he wondered what kind of wife she would make.

He stopped his mind there as he looked ahead again, catching his wayward thoughts. *You're running too far ahead of yourself,* he thought, centering his concentration back on the final song. *Way too far.* Besides, what kind of husband would he make? A simple laborer in her bakery, dependent on her for his income.

That was not what he had envisioned for any relationship he wanted to be a part of.

He turned his attention back to the service as it wound to its end. Then, as they walked out of the sanctuary, Grandpa going one way, Brian and Melissa going another, Brian caught a knowing smile from Miss Coraline, who was standing across the aisle from them.

Gossip was one of Bygones's chief forms of entertainment. He knew people would be associating him with Melissa after this. Again he caught himself feeling a mixture of frustration with his grandfather for putting him in this situation and a sense of rightness in being with Melissa.

"So the picnic is at Bronson Park?" she asked, throwing the question over her shoulder as she walked ahead.

"Yeah. It's happening right away. I figured on just walking over there. We may as well go together." Brian told himself he was just being polite.

"That would be nice. I'm still learning who is who here," Melissa said with a relieved smile.

See? It was the neighborly thing to do, Brian tried to convince himself as he and Melissa walked side by side out of the church, then down the sidewalk toward Bronson Park.

But as he glanced down at her, the sunshine bringing out the highlights in her hair, his feelings were more than neighborly.

It's a beautiful day, he told himself. *You're with a beautiful girl. Leave all the other complications back in the bakery.*

Half an hour later they sat in the shade of a large oak tree, balancing plates holding bowls of chili, biscuits and slices of pizza. Children wove in and among the people, screaming and laughing and full of the exuberance of being outside and set free from the confines of church.

"Are you sure I shouldn't have brought anything?" Melissa asked as she took a bite of the pizza she had chosen. She shot him a frown. "I could easily have supplied some cakes, cookies or muffins for this."

Brian shook his head as he wiped his mouth. "The Dills do this often and certain other people bring their food also. Just enjoy being a guest for now."

"But still—"

Brian held up a warning finger. "You don't have to do it all," he said. "You do enough, and today is the only day off you get, so just appreciate it."

She gave him a quick smile, which he returned, and again the connection that seemed to spark between them grew.

"Hey, Montclair. Don't usually see you at these things."

Brian dragged his attention away from Melissa and looked up to see Don standing above him with a smirk on his wide features. Brian could have said the same thing to Don, who didn't attend church other than at Christmas and Easter.

"It's a nice day and Grandpa wanted to come," Brian responded.

"Bet you had another reason to come, though," Don said as he glanced at Melissa, his smirk growing. "Making nice with the boss never hurts your chances at work, does it?"

He had to bring that up, didn't he? Just when Brian thought he could keep that part of his and Melissa's moment together separate.

"Nice to see you here, Don." That was all Brian said, pushing down his own confused feelings about Melissa. "Heard you're working in Concordia." The Bygones buzz had it that Don had gotten a job working at a grocery store there.

Don's grin faded and he gave a tight nod. "So what else can we do for you?" Brian asked, not wanting to talk to Don when he had Melissa beside him in a peaceful, non-work environment.

"I'm getting people together for the races. My wife always organizes them," Don said. "You entering?"

Brian shook his head. "Doubtful." He hadn't come to the picnic to participate in potentially embarrassing situations.

"What races?" Melissa asked, nudging Brian.

"The usual picnic stuff," he replied, balling up his napkin and dropping it on his empty plate. "Sack races, a three-legged race. That kind of thing."

"Sounds like fun," Melissa said with a happy grin.

"Sound like a recipe for disaster," Brian returned, getting to his feet.

"Sounds like you're backing out 'cause you know you'll lose," Don taunted. "I guess working in the bakery lifting all those heavy tarts and cookies and wearing a girlie apron probably got you out of shape."

Brian stifled a sigh and a retort about toting around vegetables.

The manly part of him wanted to take Don up

on his challenge, to prove to Don that, though he wore a pink-and-white-striped apron, he was still a guy.

To prove to the woman beside him that he was tough, in charge and more than just her employee.

"Let's do it," Melissa said, jumping to her feet and grabbing Brian's hand.

He released a sigh of resignation as she dragged him along. Guess he didn't have much choice now.

They tossed their paper plates and plastic cups into an almost full garbage can, then walked over to the area marked off with ropes on the grass to show the boundaries of the race. Mayor Langston stood to one side, leaning on his cane and calling out a challenge to contestants through a bullhorn.

"First up we're having the sack race," he called out as people lined up at the starting point, laughing and jostling each other and stepping into burlap sacks. "And after that is the three-legged race, so find your partners and go to where Lexi is handing out scarves to get hitched."

Brian held back, still unsure of how badly he wanted to embarrass himself in front of Melissa. He had his pride after all, and he figured when it came to Melissa his pride had taken enough of a wallop. But Melissa had caught his hand and pulled him along. "Let's enter the three-legged race."

"Us? In the three-legged race?"

"Let me boss you around and we'll do just fine," she said with a light laugh.

"Hope you're ready for grass stains on those white pants of yours," he said, pointing to her blinding white capris.

When she had come into church this morning, he had had to do a double take. Her everyday outfit at the bakery was a white T-shirt, black pants and an apron.

Today she wore a blue, shimmery blouse gathered at the waist, an assortment of colorful beaded necklaces, white capris and impractically high black sandals decorated with colorful beads.

Pretty was his first impression.

City girl was his second.

"The only way I'll get grass stains is if I fall," she said, unzipping the side of her sandals and kicking them off. "Which I won't."

"I didn't think I'd ever see you doing something like this," Lexi Ross said, giving Brian a pointed look.

"There's a first for everything," Brian returned, taking the scarf. Without saying anything more, he bent over to tie it around his and Melissa's ankles. She might choose to go barefoot, but he was keeping his shoes on.

"Make sure you wind it around twice," Melissa said. "And not too loose. We need to stay together. Maybe we should practice. It would be best if one of us counts off so we can keep a rhythm. Kind of a one-two count. I could do that."

Brian stopped and shot her a warning glance, squinting into the sun. "Anything else you want to let me know, boss?"

She looked taken aback, then bit her lip. "I'm being bossy, aren't I? Sorry."

Brian stood and grinned down at her, accepting her apology. "That's okay, City Slicker. I know you like to boss me around, but this is a tricky race. We need to work as a team."

Melissa nodded, a hint of a dimple appearing at one corner of her mouth as she tucked her long hair behind her ears, the gold hoops she wore glinting in the sun. "In other words, you're in charge."

"Now you're clueing in," he said, returning her mischievous smile.

Mayor Langston called for all the participants in the three-legged race to step up to the line. Melissa and Brian took their place between Elwood and Velma Dill, Don and his wife and a few other participants.

"I think we've got this race," Melissa whispered.

"Don't get overconfident," Brian whispered back. "You get cocky, you lose. Stay focused on the finish line and listen to me. You grab my waist, and I'll hold your shoulders. We'll start off with our outside feet."

"Now who's being bossy?" Melissa teased as she slipped her arm around him.

"Me for a change," he returned, putting his arm around her shoulders. He looked down at her, then around at the people watching from the sidelines. He saw Miss Coraline giving him a thumbs up, Lily waving her arms and calling out their names, Tate laughing and Amanda and her sister Amy jumping up and down with joy beside her other sister, Allison. Behind them stood Josh, watching with a huge grin and his arms folded.

His people. His town.

And he stood among them with his arm around a beautiful girl. Not his boss—just a girl. The moment was so perfect, so right, he wanted to hold and savor it.

Then Mayor Langston called for them to get ready and Brian and Melissa shuffled to the starting line, holding on to each other.

"You count, okay?" Melissa said. "I'll follow your beat."

"You catch on fast," he said, giving her a quick grin. The mayor counted down then called out "go," and they were off.

"Not such big steps," Melissa said as Brian counted off, one, two, one, two. They almost stumbled, then regained their rhythm. Soon they were gaining on the Dills, then they flew past them.

People were cheering, clapping and calling out their names as they streaked down the field, Brian counting out the rhythm. Melissa misstepped and would have fallen but Brian grabbed her under the arm and hauled her up, and soon she was back in step with him.

They made it across the finish line. First.

Brian glanced behind to see Don and his wife struggling to stay together. They piled up in a heap on the ground, and the Dills passed them to come in second place, Elwood's long hair streaking out behind him like a flag.

"We did it," Melissa called out, turning to Brian and giving him a dazzling smile. Then to his utter surprise she tossed her arms around his neck and hugged him tightly.

It was just in fun, Brian knew as he responded, holding her close. Just the thrill of the win. But she held on a bit longer than necessary and pulled back a bit slower, keeping her arms around his neck as he kept his around her waist. Her expression grew serious, her eyes luminous.

Brian couldn't look away and didn't want to. Then everything around them—the park, the people—fell away and it was simply Melissa, him and this bright and shining moment. Expectation hummed between them and Brian felt himself drawing closer to her.

Then Josh clapped him on the shoulder. "Congratulations, you guys. You two make a great team."

Brian blinked, then took a breath, feeling as if he had come up for air.

"Yeah. Thanks," he said, slanting Josh a quick glance, frustration vying with relief. He had come very close to kissing Melissa in front of most of the town of Bygones.

"Good work, guys," Lily said, running up to join them. "I thought you were going to fall for sure for a minute there, Melissa, but then Brian grabbed you and away you guys went."

"Yeah. It was fun," Melissa agreed, lowering her hands from his shoulders, her hands shaking as she pressed them together.

She looked down and was about to bend over to untie the scarf but Brian stopped her. "I'll take care of that," he said, disappointed at how husky his voice sounded.

"So are you running any more races?" Lily asked.

"No. I think we'll end on a high note," Melissa said.

Brian worked at the knot and finally got it loose. He pulled the scarf off and as he straightened, he looked over at Melissa again, surprised to see her eyes on him.

"Why don't I take that scarf back?" Lily said, tugging it free from Brian's grasp. "Brian, have you seen the community garden lately?"

"Um, no."

"You should show him, Melissa. It's coming along really well."

Melissa turned to Brian and he paused, uncertainty marring the moment. "Do you want to see it?"

"Sure. Sounds good."

"Okay. Let's go then."

Melissa gave him a quick smile, then started walking toward the garden and Brian followed along behind her. He glanced at her bare feet. "You forgot your sandals," he said.

She lifted her foot, wiggling it, then shrugged. "I don't mind being barefoot," she said. "Feels free. We can get my sandals after we see the garden. I don't imagine I have to worry about them getting stolen," she added.

"Who knows? There have been a few incidents of theft going on in the town. Some vandalism."

"You're right," Melissa said, looking over her shoulder as if having second thoughts. She paused and for a moment Brian thought she was going back.

And he didn't want her to. He enjoyed being around her in this setting. Just the two of them.

Then she shrugged. "I don't think black zip-up sandals would be a big-ticket item for a thief."

"Not like power tools," Brian returned with a sigh.

"Have you heard anything more about them?" she asked, touching his arm in a gesture of sympathy.

Brian shook his head. "Nope." Then he looked down at her and decided he didn't want to talk about power tools or Bygones or the bakery.

Her hand slid down his arm. As it reached his hand, he gave one twist of his wrist and, as if it was the most natural thing in the world, caught her hand in his.

And she let him.

They walked in silence toward the garden following the shade of the trees lining the park, a gentle summer breeze easing the warmth of the afternoon sun. Their walk took a few twists and turns and soon the sound of the picnic was behind them and the garden was forgotten.

"I'm glad we won the race," Melissa finally said. "I didn't want to get grass stains on my pants."

Brian chuckled, swinging her hand. "We worked as a team."

Melissa laughed and looked up at him. "We *are* a team. A good team. In a few other ways, too."

Brian stopped and faced her. "What do you mean?"

"When you help me in the bakery, we work well together."

Brian's only reply was a quick nod.

She frowned at his response. "You don't think we work well together?"

They did but only when he did what she told him to do. "I don't want to talk about the bakery," he said quietly.

"Why not?" Now it was her turn to frown.

"Because right here, you're just Melissa Sweeney and I'm just Brian Montclair."

Her frown deepened. "Isn't that what we are in the bakery, too?"

A stray breeze lifted a strand of her hair, dropping it across her face. He gave into an impulse and brushed it away, his touch gentle on her soft cheeks. "In the bakery, you're the boss," he said quietly. "I'm the employee, and I don't like that situation so much."

"But you enjoy working in the bakery, right?"

He lifted his shoulder in a shrug of resignation, his hand now resting on her shoulder. "I do enjoy it," he said, realizing to his surprise that this was true. "I never thought I would."

"You were a most reluctant employee," she said with a grin.

"Not going to lie," he admitted, "Wearing a pink-and-white-striped apron and baking bread was not what I saw as my future."

"And now?" Her eyes shone up at him with an expectant light, as if she hoped he shared her vision for the future.

He weighed that thought a moment, not sure he wanted to tell her that he couldn't hitch his wagon to her star. That he still had his own dreams of being in charge of his own life. Either by way of getting his job back at the factory, or starting up his mechanic shop again.

He cut that thought off. His tools were still gone. The only other "or" was driving a truck in Junction City. He wasn't that far. Not yet. He still was clinging to the hope that Mr. Randall would reopen the factory and his life would return to the normal he so craved.

When that happened, he felt he could be on a better footing with Melissa.

Then he looked down at her, his heart giving a slow thump as she smiled up at him. As he looked into her eyes, anticipation lingered. Then in spite of his own trepidation he did what seemed the most normal thing in the world at the moment.

He bent his head, touched his lips to hers and kissed her.

She released a gentle sigh, then kissed him back, twining her arms around his neck. He wrapped his arms around her tiny waist, pulling her close.

This was right, he thought, feeling her heart beating against his chest, stifling his own misgivings.

Chapter Ten

Melissa sat on her bed and leaned back against the wall, the screen of her phone glowing in the dark of her room.

She should go to bed, she kept telling herself, but after Brian had brought her back to her apartment and had kissed her good-night, she fairly floated through the door.

She had gotten ready for bed, smiling at her flushed cheeks, her mind ticking over the surprising events of the day.

Then, as she walked into her bedroom, her phone dinged and when she checked it, she saw Lily had sent her some pictures from the picnic. So Melissa had dropped onto her bed, her finger flicking over the screen of her phone as she scrolled through the pictures. She and Brian getting ready to run, the two of them starting out, stumbling. Another one of Melissa almost falling. Then the last one, at the finish line.

Her favorite one.

In the photo her hair was a tangle of copper and her face was flushed as she looked up at Brian, who was looking down at her. His arm was still around her waist, his hair also mussed, falling over his forehead and glinting in the sun.

But what caught her attention was the grin on his face. Genuine, full of life and joy. And he was smiling down at her.

Her heart gave another thump as she enlarged the picture so she could see only his face. Tiny shivers chased each other up her spine as she thought of his kiss later on, how he had held her close, how easily they fit together.

They belonged together.

No sooner had that thought formed than she felt the usual resistance. The usual caution. Did she dare take this further?

It's different, a contrary voice said. He's different.

And he was, she thought, tracing his face with her index finger. He was the first guy she had spent any time with, or been attracted to, who had a strong solid faith. Who had a solid grounding in family and community.

That created a strong attraction, but it also made her afraid.

He could be the one.

She lowered the phone, dropping her head against the wall behind her as she looked around the tiny apartment. It was a bachelor suite, utilitarian and plain. It had come furnished, so she hadn't put too many of her own touches here. A few pictures she had brought with her from her furnished apartment in St. Louis and a couple of knick-knacks she had gathered in her wanderings with her mother.

Only the few things she could toss into a suitcase.

This place, however, would be her home for longer than the six months her mother had ever stayed in one place. Longer than the year and a half she had spent in St. Louis after Jason left her hanging. The same amount of time she had spent going to school and even then she still moved every year as roommates came and went.

Here, Melissa had a two-year commitment to her business and no intention of leaving after that.

Bygones was her new home.

And Brian?

She tested the thought, as she sunk back into her pillow, her hand coming up to touch her lips.

Brian was becoming intertwined in her life here in Bygones. In spite of their rocky start, or maybe because of it, he was becoming more important to her with every day.

Her old fears and insecurities returned. Did she dare open herself up to him? Make herself vulnerable again?

Her questions grew jumbled and scattered as sleep slowly beckoned.

As she drifted off, the memories of Brian's kiss lingered and teased.

"Did you truly make this?" Coraline held up a loaf of bread and glanced toward Brian.

"I did," he said, leaning on the bakery's counter by the cash register. "Made that raisin bread, too."

Coraline gave him a smile full of satisfaction. "So, you're settling in here then."

"I like the work," he admitted. Then he added a self-conscious grin. "Plus me and Grandpa get all the bread and pastries we want for free."

And I spend every day with Melissa.

That thought reverberated, bringing with it the usual confusion. Being with Melissa every day was probably the best, and at the same time the most distracting, part of this job.

"I have to admit, it was a long shot putting your name on the list of people to work here," Coraline said as she picked out another loaf of whole wheat bread. "But I'm glad to see my instincts about you were correct."

"What instincts were those?" Brian asked, puzzled.

"That you can rise to any occasion given you."

Brian glanced behind him to where Melissa was working, humming while she put together another batch of pound cakes for the farmer's market on Saturday.

She looked up and smiled at him, and as it had every day since Sunday, awareness arced between them. He quickly turned away, hoping Miss Coraline didn't see the flush working up his neck.

"*Almost* any occasion, Miss Coraline," he said wryly as he rang in her purchases.

Miss Coraline frowned. "What do you mean by that?"

Brian just shrugged, not sure how to articulate the mixture of emotions Melissa created in him. He was not sure he wanted to bring everything out in the open and examine it yet.

For now, it seemed he and Melissa were moving somewhere. He just wasn't sure where it would all end up. "At any rate, you and Melissa seem to be getting along. You two seemed cozy on Sunday," Coraline pressed, pulling his attention back to her.

"The picnic was fun." The thought of the kiss he and Melissa had shared still created a quick lift of his heart. "We did well on the three-legged race."

"You two make a good team," Miss Coraline said, handing him the correct amount for her bread purchase.

Brian started. What Miss Coraline said echoed, almost verbatim, what Josh had said.

A team? Hardly.

"Thanks for coming to Sweet Dreams," he said, handing her the bag. "Hope to see you again."

Coraline took the bag, her expression growing suddenly serious. "Melissa seems a lot happier than when she first came here," she said, lowering her voice as she stepped closer to the counter, her expression softening. "I just want you to be careful with her. She's a lot different from the girls I've seen you dating." Miss Coraline's voice took on a peculiar tone.

"Are you warning me?" he asked, beating back a sharp tick of disappointment.

Coraline shrugged. "Maybe. A little bit. You've always been drawn to a more traditional girl. Not the kind of girl who would choose a career."

Brian wasn't sure what to make of her comment, but at the same time Miss Coraline's words created a barb of unease that resurrected his own suppressed concerns. It was true that Melissa was far more independent than anyone he'd ever been attracted to. This bakery was important to her and she poured time and energy into it.

Just then another thought occurred. Would this bakery be more important to her than anything else in her life?

He shot a glance over his shoulder just as Melissa looked up from the batter she was pouring into the cake pans. They shared a smile and in spite of his concerns, Brian again felt that peculiar connection he had never shared with anyone else.

He turned back to Coraline and gave her a noncommittal smile. "We'll have to see how things develop, won't we?"

"Of course you will." She held her bag close. "I'll be thinking of you two and praying for you."

"Thank you," he said, truly appreciative of the support.

The door opened and Joe Sheridan came into the bakery, wearing his uniform, his radio squawking on his shoulder. He tipped his hat to Miss Coraline, then held the door open for her as he muttered a response into the radio's mike.

As the door closed behind her, Joe finished his conversation, then strode over to the counter.

The solemn look on Joe's face didn't create confidence.

"I'm guessing you haven't found the tools," Brian said.

Joe shook his head. "Nor any lead on who could have taken them. But I finally have a police report ready so you can make a claim with the insurance company."

"That's a start."

"Mr. Sheridan, how are you today?" Melissa came to the front of the bakery, wiping her hands on a towel.

"Busier than a termite in a sawmill," he said, tugging at his hat. "Seems to be a spate of vandalizing going on."

"I'm sorry to hear that," Melissa said.

"Bygones is still a safe place," Joe said, holding up a hand as if to reassure her. "We'll get to the bottom of this—don't you worry."

"I'm sure you will," Melissa replied.

"In the meantime my wife sent me here with a list of things I need to pick up for some party she's having on Friday." Joe pulled a paper out of his pocket and glanced at it, then frowned. "Nope, not that one."

While he looked for the list, Melissa laid a hand on Brian's arm. "I'm going home to sleep for an hour or so. When Amanda comes, get her to mix up another batch of gingersnap cookies and put in that order I pulled together."

Brian glanced down at her, the sight of her drawn face creating a surprising upswing of protectiveness. "You go. Get some rest," he said giving her a careful smile. "I'll keep an eye on the loaves."

She frowned a moment. "Do you think I made too many? Are you sure this will work?"

"What will work?" Joe asked, holding up a bedraggled and wrinkled piece of paper Brian suspected was the stray grocery list.

"We're putting up a table at the Concordia Farmer's Market this Saturday," Brian told him.

"I hear that's a good market. Very well attended." Joe grinned at Melissa. "And your baked goods are the best I've ever eaten." He shot a quick glance around, then leaned forward, holding his hand up by his mouth as if shielding what he had to say. "Don't let my wife know I said that."

The sound of Melissa's laughter brought a smile to Brian's face. "I won't tell a soul." The she turned her smile on him. "I'll see you later," she said, then left.

Brian watched her go, but as he took care of Joe's order, Miss Coraline's words niggled back into his mind.

You've always been drawn to a more traditional girl.

That was true enough, but how much different was Melissa? Surely someday she would want to have children. To be home with them while her husband went off to work, right?

He tried to put a brake on his thoughts. He was running ahead of himself and his own warnings to take things as they came with Melissa.

Yet as he helped Joe with his order he couldn't help but wonder what Melissa would choose if the time came. Her bakery or a family.

"Best banana loaf you'll ever taste." Brian presented the cellophane-packaged loaf as one would a bottle of fine wine to the young woman standing in front of the table Melissa and Brian had set up at the farmer's market.

"I want one of those, Mommy," the little girl with her curly hair barely peeking over the table said and pointed a chubby hand at the cake pops Melissa had displayed beside a bouquet of white lilies and pink gerberas.

Lily, in the hopes of advertising her own business, had supplied the arrangements that complemented the white-and-pink-striped cloth Melissa had used to cover the table Brian had supplied. Their table wasn't as elaborate as some with their banners and tents, but Melissa felt she and Brian had a pleasant and unified presentation for their first time at the farmer's market.

"Of course, honey," the woman said. She looked over the empty spaces on the table, frowning. "You don't have much stock left."

"It's been a busy day," Melissa said, setting out the last of the loaves of apricot bread.

It was almost three o'clock, and ever since the market had opened at ten o'clock, the number of people coming through the market had slowly increased and their stock had steadily decreased.

Now, the buzz of conversation and laughter and the sound of hawkers competing with each other for people's attention created an energy that made Melissa smile. The market was set up in a park with the choice booth sites placed in the shade of the large, spreading oak trees dotting the open space. Most had brightly striped canopies with their names emblazoned on a banner across the top; some had a simple tent to shade their wares and customers from the sun.

She and Brian, newcomers to the market, were sent to the farthest corner, against the parking lot and out in the open. But in spite of being one of the most remote tables, they had done a brisk business.

"We'll have to bring more stuff if we do this

again," Brian said tucking the cash the woman had given him in the large metal box he had on a stand under the table.

"I'm still amazed we've sold as much as we have so quickly."

"You've got some unique goods to offer. Giving out samples was a genius idea. It created some good word of mouth." Brian gave her a quick smile before he turned to their next customers, a couple of women who were eyeing the tarts Melissa had set out.

While he was busy, her phone sent out a quacking sound, meaning that Amanda was returning Melissa's text. As Melissa pulled her phone out of her pocket, she turned away from him and texted Amanda back. Melissa had been texting Amanda all morning making sure everything was okay at the bakery. A couple of times Brian had threatened to take her phone away. This was the first time she had been away from the bakery, however, and she was concerned.

Brian shot her a frown as she slipped the phone into her pocket, but then he turned his attention back to the women who were hovering by his end of the table.

"What can we do for you beautiful ladies?" Brian asked, resting his hands on the table.

Melissa wanted to roll her eyes. He was lay-ing it on a bit thick, but the women laughed, ignoring her when Brian told them who had made the cakes and tarts they were admiring.

He chatted with them, telling them what items were still available. He made sure to point out the flower arrangements Lily had made and encouraged them to take her business card. As Melissa watched him engage with the women, she suspected that his blue eyes that crinkled at the corners, his strong jaw enhanced by a shadow of stubble, his broad smile and even broader shoulders were a part of the reason they were doing such good business.

As one of the women laughed, tossing her head in a frankly flirtatious gesture, Melissa couldn't help a flare of jealousy, which surprised her. Then Brian looked her way, his expression softened and she got what she, at one time, had wished for—a genuine smile.

She felt her cheeks flush in response, and she turned back to the van to take out the last pies and the last set of tarts. They had borrowed the van from Miss Ann Mars. Brian had fixed it up in exchange for being able to use it from time to time.

The women left and Brian whistled a happy tune as he put the cash in the box, then looked around over the milling crowd as if seeking out new customers.

"You're enjoying this, aren't you?" Melissa asked in a teasing voice as she closed the cooler. She tried to keep her tone light, but her previous moment of insecurity, when Brian was laughing with those women, surprised and dismayed her. Though things were shifting between her and Brian, she felt she had left herself enough of an emotional buffer. A space she could retreat to if she felt too vulnerable.

But Brian seemed to be working his way closer and closer to her heart. The thought excited and scared her at the same time.

"I like interacting with people in this kind of setting. It's less formal and more fun than in the bakery." He nodded, giving her a quick wink. "But best of all, I get to work alongside you."

As he spoke he had lowered his voice and taken a couple steps closer, creating a quiet intimacy. He threaded her fingers in his and as their eyes held she felt anticipation rise in her chest.

Melissa turned away from him and was surprised to see her hands trembling as she fussed with the table, sweeping off a few errant crumbs, needlessly adjusting the wares. Busy work, she realized. Work to keep her mind off her reaction to Brian. She went back to the van to get some more supplies, a tiny feeling of uncertainty marring the afternoon.

Shouldn't she be more careful? Shouldn't she keep her focus on her bakery?

She sent up a quick prayer for wisdom. Guidance. And when she returned to the table, she felt a little calmer.

"Well, that's the last of what we brought," she said, as she set out the last two pies and a couple of cakes.

"That's great. I was hoping we'd be done early," Brian said.

She was about to ask why when her phone buzzed again and she turned, taking a quick peek at it.

It was Amanda returning her text as Melissa had requested, telling her that everything was fine.

"How much for the pie?" an elderly man asked her, drawing her attention away from her phone.

When she told the customer the price, he frowned, his thick grey eyebrows pulling together like two small caterpillars. "Another lady, a few tables down, is selling hers for two bucks less," he griped, tugging on an equally gray beard.

"She must be doing a good business," Brian put in, coming to stand beside Melissa.

"Naw. Still has a bunch left. I bought one last week. They're not that good."

"That's too bad," Brian said. "These, however, are amazing pies. The kind of pie that makes you lie awake at night wishing you'd bought two instead of one. The kind of pie that, when you do fall asleep, will give you sweet dreams."

Melissa stifled a quick chuckle, still surprised at this side of Brian. Lighthearted, quick with words and smiling.

"I make them with fresh ingredients," Melissa put in, realizing how prosaic she sounded compared to Brian. "And they're a full inch larger than conventional pies."

"So you get more pastry and less penitence," Brian put in.

The man chuckled at that, obviously won over. He bought two, which cleaned them out of pies.

Ten minutes later all their stock was gone and she and Brian were taking down their table. A few more people stopped by, expressing their regrets. Brian promised they'd be back in two weeks with more Sweet Dreams goodness, adding that if they didn't want to wait, they could come to Bygones and get whatever they wanted whenever they wanted.

A few people promised to do just that and Melissa felt a strong sense of gratification that her mandate with the SOS Committee was being fulfilled.

And it was all thanks to Brian.

As they dismantled their site, they made plans on what they would do to improve the display. As they drove away from the park, Melissa settled back in the seat of the borrowed van, a heavy cash box sitting at her feet, a feeling of satisfaction settling on her heart. "I think that was worth our while," she said, watching the houses of Concordia slip past. Homes.

She felt a yearning for the same thing, a place of her own. Then she looked over at Brian, feeling a curious sense of anticipation.

"Of course it was. Your stuff was a hit," Brian said as he negotiated another turn.

"You helped me prepare it," she said. "You can take as much credit."

Brian shrugged off her compliment. "All I did was follow your instructions."

"But you followed those instructions so well."

"It's what I do best these days," he said with a light sigh.

She shot him a concerned glance, wondering what he meant by that, but then he gave her a quick smile and she felt it again—a sense of contentment and something she had never felt around any other guy before.

Peace.

"Are you in a rush to get back to Bygones?" Brian asked, slowing down at the corner that would take them to the highway out of town.

"Not really."

"'Cause I'm starving and man cannot live on apricot bread alone, so I was wondering if you want to go out for lunch."

The thought created a quiver of expectation. "Where…where would we go?"

"There's a cool Italian restaurant here in Concordia that my mom and dad used to go to on their anniversary. The food is great and filling."

"Sure. Sounds good." She looked over at him, pleased at the sense of contentment she felt around him. It was like they fit together. They belonged together.

The realization hit her like a burst of light.

"What are you smiling at?" Brian asked, his gaze ticking from her to the road ahead.

She hesitated, wondering if she dared articulate what she was feeling. Then her mind ticked back to that moment in church and afterward at the picnic when she and Brian raced and crossed the finish line together.

The kiss they shared.

She looked over at him, warmed by the light of his interest. "I want to thank you for your idea. Of coming to the farmer's market here. It was a great idea."

"Thanks. I'm glad it worked out." He shot her a quick smile.

"It worked out to be fantastic. I think we're creating some good word of mouth not only for the bakery but also for Lily's business."

"And hopefully the others," Brian added.

Melissa caught her lip between her teeth. "I have to apologize for underestimating you. For not listening to you and your suggestions."

"So you'll rethink the doughnut suggestion?"

She laughed. "I wasn't expecting that, but I might."

"I think you should. Doughnuts are basic and inexpensive to make other than the initial outlay for equipment. They're a bakery staple. Many group functions like to supply them with coffee. Could be another good sideline."

"Sounds like you've done some homework on this," she said, pleasantly surprised at his initiative.

He shrugged. "Yeah. Some. Guess I was just trying to prove a point."

She held his gaze and a surprising feeling of connection braided with attraction rose between them. *This matters to him. My bakery and my bakery's success matter to him.*

The idea rested in her mind and created a sense of a place in which their being together was a hope to cling to.

"You look like you just discovered a new recipe," Brian said, his gaze ticking from her to the road ahead.

"I feel like I have discovered something."

She looked over at him, warmed by the light of his interest. "You're the first guy I've ever been with who creates this sense of well-being in me. The first guy who makes me feel…right. Complete."

"In spite of how we started out?" he asked, a teasing grin edging his mouth.

"I think it might even *be* because of how we started off," she said choosing her words as carefully as she would the spices for a cake. "You pushed back. You didn't let me walk all over you the first time we met."

"Can't say I'm so proud of the pushing back," Brian said with a sheepish grin. "I wasn't the nicest guy the first time we met. I was in a funk."

"I don't blame you for that," she said quietly. "Now that I'm getting to know Bygones better, I realize seeing the money going to out-of-town people who didn't have as much invested in Bygones as you did must have been hard."

Brian was silent as he made another quick turn and parked in front of a small brick building with red curtains at the front windows. Wrought-iron tables and chairs shaded by red-

and-white umbrellas dotted the front patio. Huge pots, overflowing with white-and-red petunias and greenery, flanked the doorway.

As Brian switched off the engine, the scents of cheese, yeasty dough and garlic wafted into the van. Melissa felt her mouth water.

"It was hard to see the money parceled out the way it was," he admitted, his expression thoughtful. "But I'm also figuring out why. You have ideas I don't think anyone else would have attempted and they're working." He reached out and took her hand in his, squeezing it in a gesture of affirmation. "When I saw how people stopped by our booth at the market, how they would smile when they saw your cake pops and your tarts and the amazing things you do with bread, I realized you were what Bygones needed. A breath of fresh air and a bunch of new ideas."

Melissa was momentarily taken aback at his little speech, then she released a gentle laugh. "But, Brian, the whole reason we were even at that farmer's market was because of you. It was your idea."

He tilted his head to one side, a grin tugging at one corner of his mouth. "Yeah. I guess so."

"I wouldn't have thought of it because I don't know the area and don't know what is available." Then a thought struck her. "Maybe that's another reason the SOS Committee wanted people from Bygones to be hired. Not only to give the town employment, but to help the owners of the business see the town through their eyes."

Brian nodded slowly, as if absorbing this piece of information. "Could be."

"And you've been an asset in many other ways. I know since you started business has picked up."

"I doubt that's because of me," he protested, flipping a dismissive hand.

Melissa gave him a coy look. "Oh, I think it is. Just like we seemed to get quite a few women coming to our table today to 'buy' stuff," she said, hooking her fingers to make air quotes. "They weren't just coming for pies and cake pops."

"I think you're 'exaggerating' a bit," he said, making his own air quotes. "And now, I don't know about you, but I'm hungry. Shall we go in?" He gestured toward the restaurant.

She had her door opened by the time he came around to her side of the van, and as she was about to get out, he took her hand and helped her down.

"I can get out of a van by myself. I'm not that tired."

"I know you're not. I'm just doing what my daddy taught me."

"Country manners?" she teased, still holding his hand as they walked up the bricked path and past the flower pots.

"Manners, period," he said, opening the door of the restaurant for her. "I like to take care of the women in my life."

He gave an exaggerated bow as he stepped aside for her to enter.

Cool air washed over them, a welcome respite from the heat of the day, and Melissa blinked, her eyes adjusting from the bright sunlight to the darker interior.

"Looks like a lovely place," Melissa said, glancing around.

High wooden booths flanked one wall of the restaurant, the rest of it taken up with wooden tables and mismatched chairs. Small pots of flowers, yellow, white and red, dotted the tables. The walls were exposed brick, aged and painted with tendrils of ivy and bright red flowers.

A young woman wearing a white shirt and black skirt walked toward them holding large white menus. "Welcome to Adagio's," she said with a welcoming smile. "For two?"

"In the back courtyard, please," Brian said.

She nodded, escorted them halfway down the restaurant, then opened a side door. They entered a walled-in courtyard, large overhanging trees shading the two small wrought-iron tables sitting on the bricked patio. Red-and-white-striped umbrellas added more shade to the tables.

As the waitress set the menus down on the table, Brian pulled out a chair for Melissa. She was touched by the courtly gesture and gave him a coy smile.

The waitress lingered a moment, telling them the specials, her eyes on Brian the whole time. "Can I get you anything else?" she asked.

"Melissa, would you like some water, iced tea, coffee?" Brian asked, looking pointedly at her.

"Just some sweet tea, please."

"Make that two," Brian said, giving the waitress a polite smile, then looking back at Melissa.

Their waitress nodded, then left but before she opened the door, she shot another glance over her shoulder. Brian, however, seemed oblivious to her interest.

Melissa felt a tiny thrill of pleasure at the idea that she was with this man who, it seemed, so many women found appealing.

Melissa took her menu and opened it, but Brian left his closed on the table.

"Aren't you having anything?" she asked.

"I always get the gnocchi," Brian said, folding his arms on the small table and leaning closer, his fingers touching her arm. "I recommend it."

Melissa glanced over the items, trying to concentrate while Brian's finger traced tiny circles on her forearm. "Don't you want to try something different? There's such a variety to choose from."

"When I find something I like I stick with it."

"That's a good thing," she said quietly, her eyes meeting his.

His grin created those appealing crinkles at the corners of his blue eyes, deepening and enhancing them. "I'm a basic person. What you see is what you get." His expression grew serious as if he was about to say something else.

Then a playful breeze tossed a few errant leaves around the courtyard and lifted a strand of hair loose from Melissa's ponytail.

She reached up to deal with it, but Brian was already tucking it behind her ear, his fingers trailing down her face. "I think you should know that I want to kiss you again," he whispered.

Melissa's heart pounded against her ribs, stealing her breath. She swallowed. "You can," she whispered. She was about to lean closer when the sound of a phone ringing came from her purse.

He blew out his breath in a sigh of exasperation as Melissa reached for it.

"Amanda's phoning now instead of texting?"

Melissa nodded.

"Let it go for once," Brian said with a light frown. "She can take care of things."

Melissa shot him an agonized glance. "But I told her to call me if something went wrong."

"I know you and Amanda have been texting all morning. What could she possibly have to tell you now?"

Melissa bit her lip, glancing from the phone to Brian, sensing his displeasure, yet knowing she couldn't leave it be.

The phone stopped ringing and she relaxed. But when it started up again, she couldn't stop herself. She dove for her purse and snatched her phone, hitting the button to connect the call. "Hello, what's happening?" she demanded.

"Something's wrong with the bread mixer," Amanda wailed into the phone. "When I turned it on this morning to swish the wash water in it, it was making funny sounds. Then it quit. I didn't want to bug you so I thought maybe it would go away, but I thought I would try it again and I think it's broken."

Melissa bit her lip, thinking. She needed that mixer going first thing Monday morning. There wouldn't be anyone available tomorrow to fix it because it was Sunday. "Okay. I'll be right there."

She disconnected and grabbed her purse. "We

need to get back to the bakery," she said to a puzzled Brian, pushing her chair back with a screech on the bricks. "I need to get the bread mixer fixed."

"What's wrong with it?" he asked, still sitting.

"I don't know. Amanda said it wasn't working."

"Tell her to get Alan or Patrick at the hardware store to have a look at it. It's just a loose belt. I fixed it the other day. It probably came loose again."

"Are you sure?"

"Yeah."

Melissa glanced from her phone to Brian, thinking what to do. "I don't think I can hand that over to someone else. I need to be there."

"I can fix it when we get back."

"What if it's something more than that? I don't dare risk it."

"So we're leaving then."

"I'd like to."

Brian pushed his own chair back. "Okay. I guess the bakery comes first," he said with a sigh of resignation.

"It's my business," she said. "It's important to me."

"Of course it is." He held her gaze, his mouth

curved in a rueful smile. "I'll go cancel our drink order."

She followed him out of the restaurant. As Brian drove away from the restaurant, she sensed his disappointment.

What else could she have done? It was her bakery and it was her job to make sure everything ran well. She didn't have any choice in that matter. Surely Brian should understand that, shouldn't he?

Chapter Eleven

"It's all under control, Mrs. Morgan," Melissa said, trying to keep the annoyed tone out of her voice. "Yes, I received the picture you emailed me and I'll definitely incorporate those designs into the cake. No, you don't need to come to the bakery." Melissa suppressed the urge to roll her eyes, aware of Brian's sardonic look as he cut up the apples. "Yes. I'll call you when the cake is done."

Melissa put down the phone, shoved her hands through her hair and dropped her elbows on the butcher block counter. "And doesn't that top my Monday morning off?" She sighed.

Brian looked over from the apples he was cutting and frowned. "I'm guessing not all is well between you and Wilson Wedding World?"

Melissa blew out her breath and shook her head. "Mrs. Morgan is growing more demanding every day and that's saying a lot because she was demanding from the beginning."

"Be glad she didn't corner you at church," Brian said.

Melissa shot him a quick smile. She *was* glad. Yesterday she and Brian had attended church together, then returned to his place for lunch. But afterward Melissa was tired so Brian brought her back home.

Now it was late Monday afternoon and Melissa had returned from her apartment when Mrs. Morgan called to make sure Melissa had received an extensive email complete with pictures detailing some changes she wanted made to the wedding cake.

"Soon it will all be over," Brian assured her, finishing up his job and turning to wash his hands. "Hopefully tomorrow Amanda will be back. It's been busy today."

Melissa walked over to the bowl of apples he had cut up and frowned. "Didn't you peel the apples?"

"These are for my mom's muffin recipe." Brian dried his hands and hung the towel neatly back up on the rack.

"But I always peel apples for every recipe."

"My mother didn't for this one."

"I would prefer if you did for muffins we're selling in the bakery," she replied.

"The peel gives the muffins more fiber and adds a nice little crunch," he said picking up the bowl and dumping them in the batter and grinning at her like he was challenging her.

"Um…didn't you hear me?" She released a light laugh, her frustration with Mrs. Morgan spilling over to him but at the same time unable to stay angry with him.

He pretended to cup a hand over his ear and she chuckled.

"I know you heard me. So why did you put those apples in, anyway?"

"You only said you preferred it if I peeled them. I assumed you were giving me your personal preference."

"Well, not really. It was kind of an order."

"Which I would have ignored," he said, turning on the mixer. "Sometimes, City Slicker, you're not always right." He touched the tip of her nose, grinning as if this was some kind of joke, then he brushed a strand of hair away from her face and dropped a kiss on her forehead.

In spite of the tingle the kiss gave her, she still felt a brush of indignation at how he had ignored her "preferences."

"But it's my bakery," she said, her words coming out more forcefully than she intended.

Brian straightened, his smile dropping from

his face as quickly as his frown appeared. "Of course it is."

His mouth was set in a firm line and regret followed her impulsive words.

Then just as she was about to apologize, he turned the mixer on. "And it's my mother's recipe and we're making it her way."

Melissa dropped her hands on her hips as if to emphasize her point. "And it's my reputation that's on the line if people don't like the muffins."

"You won't quit, will you?" he said, turning to grab the papers to line the muffin pans.

"Neither will you."

He set the papers down and looked at her. Then to her surprise he took a finger full of dough from the mixer and flicked it at her.

As a small portion of it landed on the front of her apron she could only stare at him, then at the dough now dripping down a pink stripe. "What are you doing?" She ripped off a paper towel and wiped it off.

He shrugged. "Worked for us last time we had a fight."

She stared at him trying to think what he meant. Then the memory returned and with it came a bubble of laughter. She suppressed it, still upset with him, but she couldn't stop as she remembered how silly they both looked after that cake fight.

"Is this what this is?" she asked, balling up the paper towel and tossing it in the garbage can.

Brian laughed, touched her face, his hand drifting down to her shoulder, and gently pulled her close. She melted into his embrace with a sigh of contentment. She closed her eyes, her hands curling on his chest, the insecurities she usually felt fading further and further into the recesses of her mind.

Possibilities danced within reach.

Her and Brian.

"I think we have to stop meeting like this," Brian chuckled, his voice a rumble beneath her cheek. "I think we might have to make sure Amanda takes a few more days off."

"It would make us busier," she whispered.

"But give us more privacy," he returned, stroking her hair.

She lifted her face and as she did, he kissed her. She felt as if her heart had found a home, as if the dreams she had dreamed all her life were slowly coming true.

The independence of her own business, a man who cared for her and a place in a community she was slowly feeling a part of.

"Hello, is anyone here?"

Melissa drew back, disconcerted at the sound

of the tremulous voice. "That's Gracie Wilson," she whispered.

"She doesn't sound good," Brian said. "Better go see what she wants."

Melissa found Gracie standing in the middle of the store, twisting the ends of her oversize brown plaid shirt around and around her hands. From the look of the dust on it and her faded jeans, she had been working in the back of the hardware store.

When Gracie saw Melissa, she managed an unsteady smile. "Hey, Melissa."

"Hey yourself. How are you doing?"

Gracie blinked and drew in a long, slow breath. "I'm okay. I think." Then she shook her head and dropped her head into her hands. She didn't look okay.

Melissa walked around the counter, put her arm around Gracie's shoulder and led her to the back of the bakery. She set her down on a chair and kneeled beside her.

"What's wrong?"

Gracie dragged her hands over her face, her body drooping on the chair. "I don't know. I'm feeling nervous and scared. I'm not sure."

Melissa shot Brian a worried look, but he only shrugged, as if uncertain what they should say.

"What aren't you sure about?" Melissa asked.

"This wedding. I need some advice."

Melissa sat back, Gracie's simple words creating a quiver of concern. "Tell me what you're feeling." Melissa was at sea here, not sure how to help. Was Gracie simply getting cold feet, or was it something more serious?

"Nervous, like I said." Gracie's teeth worked at her lower lip, her hands twisted together in her lap. "I feel like everything is coming at me at once and I can't think. Can't figure out what to do." She pressed her lips together. "I miss my mom."

"Of course you would," Melissa assured her. "What bride wouldn't want her mother around on this special occasion?"

"Yeah. But I miss her for more than that. I wish I could talk to her about how I'm feeling." Gracie sniffed, then shook her head, straightening as if putting her emotions behind her. "But I didn't come here to dump on you. I wanted to ask you about the cake. Did Mrs. Morgan say anything about it being a carrot cake with cream cheese icing?"

Melissa shook her head. "Far as I know Mrs. Morgan wants a red velvet cake with fondant."

Gracie's teeth worried her lips some more. "I told her I wanted carrot cake. It was my mom's favorite, but Mrs. Morgan ignores what I say. Every time."

Melissa and Lily had discussed how high-handed Mrs. Morgan had been with the wedding preparations and both agreed Trent should step up.

"I think you need to talk to Trent about this," Melissa encouraged.

Gracie tweaked out a lukewarm smile. "Trent doesn't seem to care much about the party stuff, as he calls it. He's been busy at work, or he says…" Her voice faded off as if she was unsure of her own defense of him. "Then yesterday he told me I didn't need to work at the hardware store anymore. That I should quit. But I can't. Business is picking up at the store and I like my job. Besides, Trent is never home, anyway. He's always gone. I may as well be working." Gracie shook her head, as if regretting her sudden outburst. "Don't mind me," she said. "I'm just out of sorts."

"You should talk to Trent. Let him know how you feel."

"He doesn't always answer his phone." Gracie rubbed the back of her neck, as if easing out the kinks in it, then stood, giving Melissa a quick smile. "Thanks for your help. I appreciate it."

"Before you go, why don't you look at what Mrs. Morgan chose for the cake? Maybe we can figure out something that will work for both of you."

She nodded, and as she followed Melissa to

her small office, the young girl looked more like she was making plans for a funeral than for a wedding.

Brian watched Melissa and Gracie leave the room. He felt bad for the poor girl but figured she was simply feeling last-minute nerves. He didn't blame Trent for not getting involved. Weddings were mostly about the bride. When Kirk got married to Abby, he had told Brian all he had to do was shut up, dress up and show up.

As he dropped mounds of muffin mix into the oversized paper cups, his mind slipped back to his own tiff with Melissa. In spite of how it ended, her attitude bugged him.

As Melissa said, it was her bakery and Brian knew that was part of his problem. He was a hired hand here and although things had changed between him and Melissa, that basic aspect of their relationship hadn't. She was his boss.

Melissa returned, frowning at the papers she held and glancing over her shoulder as the outside door fell shut behind Gracie.

"I'm concerned about that girl." Melissa set the papers on the work counter.

"She's probably just suffering from wedding jitters, and who wouldn't with Mrs. Morgan in charge?" Brian said, measuring out the mix into the muffin pans.

"So you're still going with what you made?" Melissa asked, taking a little side trip into control territory.

"If it doesn't turn out, you can take the ingredients out of my salary," he returned, trying to keep his tone light. "Just trust me and trust my mother's recipe."

"Sorry. I'll stop now," she said, lifting a hand in a gesture of surrender. "I'll reserve judgment until I try them."

"That's all I ask," he said.

Melissa looked down at the papers on the counter. "I guess I'm worried about Gracie."

"What are you worried about?"

"I'm concerned that she doesn't feel she can count on Trent to back her. From the sounds of things, she can't count on him to take her side with her future mother-in-law. If he can't do that, I'm wondering if he's the right person for her."

"Trent's okay," Brian assured her. "All the women in town agree that he's a good catch. He makes good money. She'll be able to give up her job at the hardware store and he'll be able to provide her with a life of leisure."

Which was more than he could do for any

future wife of his. At least Trent could provide for his family on his own.

You will, too.

"I don't think Gracie is eager to give up her job," Melissa said, wrinkling her forehead in a frown. "I think it's important that she have something she can count on when people around her fail."

Brian's own concerns ratcheted a notch as he guessed Melissa wasn't only talking about Gracie.

"*When* people fail?" he said.

"It happens, and a girl shouldn't have to count on other people to provide for her."

"What's wrong with having someone provide for you? Or taking care of you?"

Melissa tapped her fingers on the counter, apparently agitated. "I think a woman needs to take care of herself, and the only way to guarantee that is to make her own money."

Her impassioned words struck him at his core. As they settled, he felt as if he was hovering on the precipice of an uncertain place.

Right now she was right. She had to make her own money because he couldn't provide for her on what he made now. And he only had the job he did because of Melissa.

Brian thought of the phone call he had gotten from Kirk last night. A company based out of Concordia, affiliated with the company Kirk worked for, was looking to hire. A job there might be coming up in a couple of weeks.

Concordia wasn't as far as Junction City. He could stay in Bygones, but he would be away from home more. Which would mean leaving Grandpa alone again.

But you could make enough money to hold your head up high. To bring in the same money Melissa is bringing in.

He wanted to think it didn't matter, but it did. If he was going to be with someone, it had to be as an equal partner.

"You understand what I'm saying, don't you?" Melissa's voice took on a pleading tone. "You get what I mean?"

"I get that your independence is important to you," he replied. "You need to be in charge." He spoke the words as a statement of fact rather than a question.

"Yes."

Something inside him clenched like a fist at her single word. He picked up the filled muffin containers and carried them to the oven, his mind spinning. He wondered if she would be able to see a marriage as a partnership. Would her work come first?

What she said wasn't new to him, but her in-dependence hadn't mattered before.

Before she had become more important than any other woman in his life.

Chapter Twelve

The bell for the front door sounded just as her office phone rang. Melissa walked away to answer the phone, and Brian set the timer for the muffins, then walked to the front of the bakery to do his job—take care of customers.

A tall man with a head full of salt-and-pepper hair and wearing a golf shirt and khaki pants stood with his hands clasped behind his back, looking at the window display Melissa and Amanda had put together. Amanda had found some old Bygones school yearbooks, designed a banner in support of keeping the school open and made a display around them.

"This is a great idea," the man was saying. "Supporting the school like this. I hope it works out."

Brian felt a jolt of shock and surprise as he recognized his former boss, Robert Randall.

The last time Brian saw Mr. Randall the man had looked haggard and worn as he handed Brian his pink slip.

But today Robert Randall looked much happier and as Brian saw his grin, hope swooped through him. Had Mr. Randall come to tell Brian that the factory was opening again? That he too had been the recipient of the grant money handed out to people like Melissa?

His former boss's visit to the bakery coming so close on the heels of his own thoughts created a hope Brian hadn't felt in a long time.

Things were going to be okay.

"Good afternoon, Mr. Randall," Brian said with a wide grin. "What can I do for you?"

Mr. Randall frowned as he glanced at Brian, surprise flickering on his expression. "So what are you doing here?" Mr. Randall asked.

"I work here now," Brian said.

"Quite different from your work at the plant, I imagine," Mr. Randall said, looking around at the display cases full of pastries and pies and the racks of bread that Brian had baked this morning. "Very different." Brian mentally compared the muffins he had just made to supervising heavy equipment worth hundreds of thousands of dollars. His old job had required planning, fast thinking and organizational skills. Manly work. The kind of work Brian excelled at.

"Funny how our lives take these twists and turns and the good that comes out of it," Mr. Randall said with a smile that reignited Brian's spark of hope.

"Good?"

Mr. Randall nodded. "The factory was such a huge part of my life and I've done what I could to get the factory going again."

Going again.

A weight Brian had been carrying since he walked out of the plant with a pink slip in his pocket finally slipped off his shoulders when he heard those words. Mr. Randall was starting up the factory again and Brian would get his old job back. He could come to Melissa on equal terms. He wouldn't be her employee anymore.

He could make plans for a future.

"That's great," Brian said, feeling like a kid at Christmas. "I'm so glad to hear that."

"Unfortunately, it wasn't enough," Mr. Randall continued. "I've decided to cut my losses while I still have some equity in the place. I'm putting the land and the buildings up for sale."

The words fell with a heavy thud.

"What? Selling the land? Closing the factory for good?" Brian's brain doubled back as he struggled to keep up with what Mr. Randall was saying. "You're walking away from it?"

Mr. Randall's decisive nod extinguished the last spark of Brian's hope.

"That factory cost me more than I can begin to count," he said quietly. Brian wondered if Mr. Randall was talking about the divorce he had just endured.

"However, that wasn't the main reason I came here today," Mr. Randall continued, giving Brian an apologetic look. "But because I ran into you here, I thought it would be best you hear it from me and not through Bygones gossip." He took a deep breath as if centering himself, then glanced at the display cases. "My biggest reason for coming was to buy some doughnuts. They weren't in stock the last time I was here."

"Still don't have any, but…but we are thinking of adding them," Brian said, clenching his fists to try to regain control of his flailed emotions. He couldn't even feel the slightest bit of satisfaction that he had been right about the doughnuts and that he and Melissa were making plans to buy the equipment. Not after the bomb Mr. Randall had dropped into his life.

"Can I…can I get you anything else?"

"What do you recommend?" Mr. Randall asked.

"The chocolate almond bars are good. Pound cakes are great. The apple tarts are always a hit." Brian ran through the list on autopilot, still trying to absorb the shock Mr. Randall's words had given him.

"I'll take a dozen of the squares and two pound cakes," Mr. Randall said, smiling as he pointed out which ones he wanted.

Brian's movements were automatic as he set the bars on a Styrofoam tray, then wrapped them in plastic. As he sealed them, he pulled in a long, slow breath.

For so long, buried in the back of his mind was the dream the factory would start up again fueled by the various rumors that had flown through the town. When Mr. Randall laid him off, Brian had hoped it was a temporary closure. Everyone thought Mr. Randall was regrouping after his divorce from his wife, Linda, last year. Having her leave him after twenty-seven years of marriage probably blindsided him and Brian thought he just needed time to adjust. There had been rumors of downsizing and maybe retooling the plant. Whitney, they reported, had said the same thing. Brian had taken this job thinking it was only a temporary measure. And now?

But you like working here.

Brian held the words a moment, recognizing the truth of them.

The smell of bread baking, the challenge of trying different recipes, the satisfaction he got from seeing the result sitting neatly on the trays with the decorative edging Melissa insisted on; all this gave him a feeling of gratification new to his life.

However, he could not escape the reality that he was still an employee working for Melissa. He had made more money working in the factory than he could ever make working in the bakery.

And in the bakery, Melissa was the boss.

"Good afternoon, Mr. Randall." Melissa's happy voice called out from behind him. "How are you doing?"

"I'm doing okay," Mr. Randall said. "I'm sorry you don't have doughnuts yet, but Brian persuaded me to try a few other items."

Melissa laughed and put her hand on Brian's shoulder. "The doughnuts are part of a future plan. I wasn't planning on carrying them, but Brian has convinced me." She smiled at him as she tightened her hand. "It's not the only good idea he's come up with."

Brian knew she didn't mean her praise to be patronizing, but that's how it felt.

"Brian is a valuable employee," Mr. Randall said. "You're lucky to have him."

"That I am," Melissa said.

"I was worried about him when he left, but I'm glad to see him settled in another job."

Brian's frustration with his situation bubbled over. He jerked his shoulder away from Melissa's hand as he took Mr. Randall's money. He gave him his purchases, mumbled an excuse, spun around and walked to the oven, ostensibly to check on his muffins. They wouldn't be ready for another four minutes, but he didn't want to stick around listening to his former boss and current boss talking about him like he wasn't even there.

Employee of the month, that's what he was, he thought, tossing the cloth he'd just used into the sink. Then he walked past the oven to the back door of the bakery. He slapped his hands against the metal bar and stepped from the heat of the bakery into the heat of the afternoon.

He leaned back against the rough stucco of the wall, thinking again of Melissa and Mr. Randall talking to each other. Each on equal footing. Each a boss of Brian.

He glanced at the park across the street, his brain spinning in circles. Mothers chatted at picnic tables nursing cups of coffee from Cozy Cup Café. Dale Eversleigh sat at another table playing chess with Elwood Dill.

The sound of kids squealing sifted over the wind toward him, creating an ache of melancholy. By this time in his life he had assumed he would have been married with a couple of kids.

He dragged his hands over his face, sending up a hasty prayer.

Please, Lord. I don't know what to do. I don't know how I'm supposed to feel.

Everything that had been normal and ordinary in his life had been swept away the past few years. His parents. The farm. His job. His plans and dreams for his own business.

Now he was dating a woman whose independence and values were opposite of everything he had hoped for in a wife. A woman who he didn't feel he could come to on equal footing.

He pulled in another breath, his duties slowly pulling at him. The muffins were probably ready, he thought, pushing himself away from the wall.

He yanked open the door and strode through the back of the bakery. Melissa stood by the worktable, muffins cooling on a rack as she took a bite of a steaming muffin.

She glanced up as he approached, looking guilty. She licked an errant crumb off her lip. "These are actually pretty good," she said, leaning against the table and trying to catch his eye. "The apple peel definitely gives the muffins another flavor and texture."

He pulled in a breath, recognizing that she was extending an olive branch, and he sensed from the puzzlement in her voice that she wasn't sure why she had to.

"Glad you like them," he said.

She returned his tentative smile.

"I have a few errands to run," she said, wiping her hands on a towel. "I'll be gone for a bit. Thought I'd let you know."

"Sure."

He knew he was being curt, but he felt as if he walked on shaky ground, not sure where his foot would land next. If he started talking, he was scared he would say the wrong thing the wrong way.

His feelings for Melissa were deep and strong. And confusing.

"Are we okay?" she asked, reaching out to him.

He took her hand, wrapping his fingers around it and struggling to articulate the mixture of feelings coursing through him. He cared for her more than he had ever cared for anyone else. He found himself wanting to make plans. Plans for a nebulous future.

But how could he think of that when he felt inadequate? When he felt he couldn't even meet her as an equal?

Something had to change, he thought, running his fingers over her knuckles. Now that Mr. Randall had delivered the death knell to the chief part of Brian's plans for the future, he would have to do what he thought he never could. Find a job outside of Bygones.

He thought of his grandfather but realized that in this situation he now had to think of Melissa.

He looked up at Melissa, then gave in to an impulse and brushed a light kiss over her forehead.

"We're okay," he said, giving her a gentle smile.

She nodded, reluctantly drew her hands out of his, then turned and walked back to her office.

Brian watched her leave the bakery, then returned to his work, his hands working automatically as he rolled out dough for cinnamon buns, a new venture for him. But all the while he worked, he struggled to sort out the events of the past few hours.

And the decisions he felt he had to make.

"Sorry I'm late," Melissa puffed, setting her iced cappuccino down with one hand and hanging her purse over the back of the chair. She and Lily had been trying to get together at the Cozy Cup Café for the past few days. It was Wednesday morning and it had finally happened. "I got waylaid on my way here by Dale Eversleigh. He wanted to know if I needed more help business-wise, that kind of thing."

He had also talked a little too long with a little too much eye contact. She hoped that somehow, somewhere he would find somebody else to turn his dubious charms on.

"They must have had a meeting of the SOS Committee last night," Lily said, taking a delicate sip from her lemonade. "Coraline stopped by the store today, too, to ask me how the business was going. I wish I could tell her that huge amounts of money are pouring in so she can give a favorable report back to the SOS Committee, but I can't. I wonder if they're getting pressure from the guy Whitney always calls Mr. Moneybags."

"Maybe. Whoever that person is." Melissa caught her worried frown. "But the shop is doing okay, isn't it?"

"Last week was slow and I have to remind myself that I can't judge how my business is doing by one week." Lily wrinkled her nose, then adjusted her glasses. "How about you?"

"The Farmer's Market did well for us," Melissa said, almost feeling guilty that her business was picking up. "Brian hit a good idea there, but it also made us busy. We're trying one in Junction City next weekend once Gracie and Trent's wedding is over."

Lily folded her arms over themselves, leaning forward. "And how are things going with you and Brian the Burly Baker?"

"I'm not sure." Melissa blew out a sigh that puffed up an errant strand of hair. "We had a fight yesterday. I think."

"About what?"

"Gracie Wilson came to the bakery yesterday and after she left Brian made some comment about how easy Gracie will have it once she's married. He got all old-fashioned and I got nervous thinking he meant any wife of his should stay home and I made some crack about needing my independence and making my own money."

Lily pursed her lips. "What did he say to that?"

Melissa shook her head, running her finger through the damp circles her cup had left on the table. "Nothing. He just clammed up and then this morning we got into a discussion about apple peel and muffins," Melissa released a light laugh, still surprised she got so huffy about something so simple. "And then he got kind of ticked and next thing I know he's giving me a kiss. I don't have a clue what he's thinking. Plus he was gone for a while yesterday and wouldn't tell me where he was going."

"It's probably nothing." Lily waved off Melissa's concerns with a flip of her delicate hand.

"Maybe he had to leave for a dentist appointment or doctor's appointment. Guys hate talking about that kind of stuff."

"Maybe I'm overreacting," Melissa agreed.

"Maybe."

Melissa took another sip of her cappuccino, still not convinced, but she didn't want to harp on her problems about trying to figure Brian out.

Their conversation roved from relationships to business to talk of Mr. Randall putting the factory and its land up for sale and what affect it would have on the town. Inevitably the chat moved back to Gracie Wilson's wedding.

"I'm worried about that girl," Melissa said, finishing her drink. "I got the feeling she's getting cold feet and now I have to find a way to tell Mrs. Morgan that Gracie wants carrot cake and not red velvet cake."

"You have fun with that." As Lily finished her drink she stood. "But I should go and do my own damage control for the Morgan wedding."

"One more week and we can go back to ordinary life," Melissa said, getting up too. Lily laughed, said goodbye and left.

Melissa glanced at her watch. She had told Amanda she would be back at two, and she still had to talk to the accountant. Then she had to post some bills at the post office and pick up the mail.

As she gathered her purse, the door of the coffee shop opened, bringing in a wave of heat from outside and Mr. Randall with it. As the door whooshed shut behind him, he glanced over and caught Melissa's eye. He smiled, walking toward her.

"Are you on your way back to the bakery? Amanda told me I needed to talk to you about a cake I want made for my daughter, Renee. I forgot to mention it when I was in on Monday."

"Sure. Let's go there now," Melissa said. She could do her other errands later.

"Renee's not a kid anymore, but I thought I would make her day special, what with all that's been happening lately." He gave Melissa a sheepish smile. "Sorry. I don't mean to dump my problems on you."

"Don't worry," she said, holding up her hand. "Let's go to the bakery and we can figure out the perfect cake for her." She tossed her cup in the garbage and gave Josh, standing behind the counter, a quick smile. "Thanks for the iced mocha latte."

Ever since their handshake agreement about her providing exclusive pastries for his coffee shop, Josh had given her her choice of free drinks. She had protested, but he insisted, telling her it was simply good business sense.

Josh acknowledged her thanks with a tight nod as he wiped his hands on a small white towel, frowning as he watched Mr. Randall leave.

Melissa felt Josh's concern. She was sure he had also heard the news of Mr. Randall's decision to sell the factory property. Like her, he was probably also wondering about the repercussions for Bygones. Though the factory had been closed for a while, Melissa was convinced there were people who had hoped it would start up again.

"Did you have any flavor in mind?" Melissa asked as Mr. Randall opened the door to the bakery for her.

"Chocolate. It's her favorite."

They walked into the bakery, and Melissa saw Brian bent over the counter writing on some papers in front of him. He looked up just as she came in, a frown deepening the set of his eyes.

Then he grabbed the papers and shoved them in an envelope, bending over to put them away. He looked guilty.

What was going on?

"Afternoon, Mr. Randall. Melissa, you're back early." He frowned. "I thought you had some other appointments."

"Mr. Randall wants a cake for his daughter." She hid her hurt as she turned to Robert. "Why don't I show you what I've done so far? I have a binder in my office we can look at."

She skirted the counter Brian stood behind, walking past him to her office with Mr. Randall following.

"Before you leave, I'd like to talk to you," Brian said.

Melissa spun around, but he was looking directly at Mr. Randall.

"Of course," Robert said.

Melissa shot Brian a puzzled glance, but he turned away without making eye contact, which bewildered her even more. Something was going on.

When she was done with Mr. Randall, he and Brian walked out of the bakery together.

Curiosity had her poking her head around the edge of her office door. All she saw was Mr. Randall standing in front of the bakery and nodding at Brian. Then Mr. Randall pulled out a business card and scribbled something on the back. He handed it to Brian, who tucked it in the back pocket of his blue jeans, glancing around as if checking to see who might have noticed.

Melissa pulled back, guilt from spying suffusing her. But she did wonder what that was all about, and why did Brian seem so furtive?

When Brian returned, Melissa shot quickly back to her desk, pretending to be engrossed in writing down the instructions for Renee's cake.

Brian walked past her office, and for a moment she wanted to call out, to ask him what was happening.

She couldn't stop the faintest tremble of fear that something serious had shifted in their relationship. Not knowing what it was made her even more afraid.

She couldn't let him know that. It would give him control over her. She didn't dare let that happen. So she said nothing.

When Amanda came back to the bakery, Melissa told her she had to run some errands and wasn't sure when she'd be back.

She kept herself away from the bakery until just before closing time, dawdling through her appointments and taking her time at the post office. She stopped at the bookstore to talk to Amanda's sister Allison and check on a book she had asked her to order. They chatted about business. Allison told her how much Amanda liked working at the bakery and asked how Brian was doing.

Melissa chose to ignore the faint innuendo in Allison's voice, then left. She stopped in at the This 'N' That to say hi to Miss Ann, who was bustling about, hanging up some new clothes she had received.

Then, when she couldn't put it off any longer, she returned to the bakery fifteen minutes past closing time. Amanda was sweeping in the back, her brown ponytail bouncing with her effort. Brian had already left.

"I'll finish up here," Melissa said to Amanda.

"Awesome." Amanda yanked off her apron with an alacrity that made Melissa smile. "Mom is teaching me and Amy to sew. Today we're cutting out a dress." She tossed her apron in the bin with the rest of the laundry, then stopped at the door, snapping her fingers. "Forgot to tell you, but Brian said he had to take off tomorrow. About ten o'clock. Something about a job he had to do."

Why hadn't Brian told her himself? What was going on?

"Of course," she said with a tight nod, as if she knew exactly what was up.

Amanda gave her a knowing grin. "I wonder if he's planning some surprise for you. He's been so secretive lately. Making phone calls in the back room and getting a ton of text messages."

Melissa brushed off her supposition, but all the same she suppressed a curl of unease. Brian had retreated from her and she doubted that what Brian was planning had anything to do with her.

"You have fun sewing your dress," Melissa said, forcing a light tone to her voice.

Amanda left and Melissa returned to her office. Weariness clawed at her and she wanted nothing more than to go to her apartment, curl up in bed and sleep.

She walked to the front of the store to double check everything was in order. Of course it was, she thought. Brian was meticulous in his cleaning and organizing.

She walked around the counter, back to her office, and as she did, she brushed against an envelope sitting on a shelf beneath the counter.

It fell to the ground and papers spilled out. Melissa crouched to pick them up, looking over them as she did. Where had these come from?

As she scanned the papers, her heart plummeted into the soles of her feet when she remembered Brian had pushed an envelope this size under the counter.

It held completed application forms for jobs in companies based in Concordia and Junction City.

Filled out by Brian.

Chapter Thirteen

The back door of the bakery opened and Melissa felt her heart jump in her chest as Brian entered. Yesterday, after finding the application forms, she had wanted to grab them, chase down Brian and ask him what was going on.

But, of course, she didn't. This morning she worked alone in the silent bakery, her heart sore. Amanda had offered to come and help, but Melissa wanted time and space to think.

She spun the cake around on the pedestal, smoothing the icing on the side with the wide spatula. She was trying hard to look in command of her wavering emotions.

She set the spatula down and filled the piping bag. "Did your appointment go okay?" she asked Brian, keeping her question vague, hoping to give him a chance to tell her.

"Yeah. It did." He grabbed his apron and tugged it over his head.

She piped the icing on the cake with swift, sure motions, then decided to stop dancing around the issue.

"So, did you get the job?"

She shot a quick look at him looming above her, his hands resting on his jean-clad hips, his cheeks still shining from his close shave this morning. His hair was tamed, brushed back from his face, emphasizing his blue eyes with their fan of lighter wrinkles holding hers with a look of surprise.

"I know you were looking for another job," she said quietly. "I thought I would come out and address it head on."

He pulled his hand over his face, sighed, then nodded. "Yes. I did get a job offer, thanks to Mr. Randall."

"Awesome." She turned her attention back to her cake, but her hand wobbled and the bead of icing she was placing on the top edge of the cake dribbled down the side. She blew out a sigh of frustration and grabbed a spatula to smooth it out. But as she picked up the errant icing, one edge of the spatula dug into the side of the cake, ruining the smooth finish.

She tossed the spatula aside and spun around, her frustration, sorrow and anger building.

"Were you going to tell me before or when you quit?" She couldn't keep the edge out of her voice, surprised herself at the anger that spilled out. "Why hadn't you told me right away what you were doing? Why did you think you needed to keep this secret?"

Brian took a step toward her, holding his hand out as if to placate her. "I was going to tell you today." He touched her shoulder and for a moment she was tempted to lean into his touch, to let him support her.

She pulled back. "Tell me why you needed to ditch working for me to find another job? I thought you liked it here."

"I'm not ditching you. I told my new boss I wouldn't be able to start for a couple of weeks. I wanted to give you time to find someone else."

She absorbed this information, unable to stifle her feeling of betrayal. "So you were just leaving me? I thought we… You and I…" She caught herself there, stepping dangerously close to asking him about the status of their relationship.

He sighed, shoving his hand through his hair, rearranging it, softening it. "I thought so, too," he said quietly. "I thought things could work the way they are. But they can't. I need some feeling of self-worth. Of pride."

As his words slid like icicles into her soul, she

flashed back to that moment of tension between them when they talked about Gracie. Brian had figured she would have been happy to quit her job and stay at home.

And before that, when they met another one of his old girlfriends, Lexi Ross. The perfect wife and mother who quit her job to take care of the children. Brian had commented on how commendable that was.

She couldn't be that kind of girl, and if Brian didn't understand that, then he didn't understand her.

And the fact that he was willing to leave her and her bakery in the lurch also showed that he didn't understand how important this was to her.

The thought sucked the center out of her world.

She thought Brian was different. Thought that she mattered to him. But it was Jason and her father all over again. None of them saw her and what she needed. They only saw what they felt they had to do. But this time, she would be the one in charge. She would determine how things went.

She looked away from him, her pain battling with her anger.

You need to be in control. You have to stop letting men have the upper hand. You have to take care of yourself.

"You don't need to stay," she said, keeping her voice low to overcome the tremble she was afraid would come into it. "In fact, if you're leaving, you may as well leave right now. I don't need your help. I don't need you."

She heard the swift intake of his breath and she knew he understood exactly what she meant. She didn't dare look at him. Didn't dare make eye contact. Because if she did, she was afraid she would change her mind.

In her peripheral vision she saw him yank off his apron and toss it onto the counter. "That's just the problem, isn't it?" he said, his words harsh with anger.

Then before she could respond to that, he spun around and strode out of the bakery.

Melissa winced at the slamming of the metallic door echoing like a shot through the room. She closed her eyes, gathering her scattered emotions, pressing her fingers against her eyes as the silence following his departure seemed to mock her.

You're all alone. Again.

What choice did she have? Should she have asked him to stay? To not take the other job? Should she have offered him a raise?

Could she have worked with someone who couldn't recognize her needs? Her dreams?

She couldn't be the woman Brian wanted,

and now Brian had gotten another job. He had left her.

You told him you didn't need him.

Melissa raised her head, looking around the bakery and trying to get her bearings.

Following Brian's suggestions, they had re-arranged some of the equipment to make a smoother workflow. Thanks to him they would be going full tilt making pound cakes, pies, squares and cake pops to take to another farmer's market at the end of next week on top of their increasing business.

She had taken his advice about the dough-nuts, and they had sat down together and figured out which machine they should buy and how big it should be.

She thought the fact that he was involved in the plans showed that he was as excited about working here as she was. Excited to be a part of what she was doing here. She truly thought she had found someone who wanted to share in her dream for a change.

She thought she had found someone who was willing to consider what she wanted and to think of it as important.

Guess she had been wrong about Brian.

Sudden, overwhelming despair washed over her and she sagged against the table, her pain and loss swirling around her soul.

But this time, her solitude had claws that clung. Brian's leaving felt like a bigger betrayal than any she had felt before. She had sensed a true growing love between them. He had helped her strengthen her faith, and sharing that bond created a deeper relationship than she'd ever had with anyone before.

And now what?

You've got your bakery, she reminded herself. *You've got what you've always wanted—a way of taking care of yourself.*

Despite her self-talk, however, it seemed pointless without Brian to share it all with.

Somehow she stumbled through the rest of the day. She called and managed to explain to Amanda that Brian had quit without choking up as she was afraid she would.

But when she got home, she sat down on her couch and allowed the tears to flow. Then, because she felt as if she had nowhere else to go, she picked up the Bible Pastor Garman had given her and opened it up to a page she had marked the other day.

And she started reading.

"You've really let this flower bed go to pot." Brian's grandfather pushed the shovel in the weed-infested dirt and turned it over.

"I'm not a gardener," Brian muttered, plunging his own shovel into the packed dirt of the bed flanking the steps of the veranda. "Especially not a flower gardener."

The late midday sun was pouring down and Brian wondered about the wisdom of working in this heat, but his grandfather was adamant they clean the flower beds while Brian had time off. Thankfully they were working in the shade thrown by the ash and maple trees that his grandfather had planted aeons ago.

After they were done here, they would drive to the community garden to help with the weeding there.

Though Grandpa hadn't said anything when Brian showed up in the middle of a working day, he figured his shrewd grandfather knew exactly what was going on. Of course, Brian was sure his frustration and anger was on display for anyone who had eyes to see.

Now, the hard, physical work helped him release some of his frustrations with Melissa. Some of his worries.

"Gardens take careful nourishing," Grandpa said, turning over another shovelful of dirt. "They need tending every day, and that's not easy to stick with."

Brian grunted in reply, wiping the sweat flowing down his forehead.

"I remember your grandmother working

every day on the flower gardens and the vegetable garden," Grandpa said, stopping to take a drink of water from the bottle sitting on the stair of the veranda. "She'd be plucking and pruning and weeding, and sometimes it seemed like she was wasting time and often she'd come into the house with scratches on her hands and broken fingernails, but the garden always looked tidy. The flowers always bright and cheerful." Grandpa released a lingering smile. "Maintenance, she always said. Steady, daily maintenance is the key to good gardens and good marriages."

Brian bent over and pulled out a particularly pernicious thistle. "Wouldn't know about the good marriage part," he said, tossing the thistle on the pile of other weeds on the grass. "Probably never will."

Grandpa was quiet a moment, then stopped again, leaning on his shovel. "You and Melissa have a falling out?"

Brian shrugged his grandfather's question away and shoved his spade in the dirt again, narrowly missing a rose bush.

"Because I kind of thought she and you were, you know, sweet on each other."

The old-fashioned phrasing made Brian smile in spite of himself. "Not so sweet anymore," he said, turning over the dirt. "I quit at the bakery."

"Why would you do that? I thought you enjoyed working there."

Brian broke up the clump of dirt with his shovel, surprised at his grandfather's bewilderment. "I did, but it was just a job until the factory opened again or I could start up my mechanic shop," Brian responded.

"You still want to do that? Have your own mechanic shop?"

Brian shrugged, testing the idea. To his surprise, since working at the bakery he hadn't thought much about mechanic work or pursued getting more.

"I'm not sure. I think it was a dream and maybe I was counting too much on the factory opening again to focus on it."

"Or maybe you were having too much fun working at the bakery to focus on it too much."

Brian shot his grandfather a frown, but Grandpa ignored him, limping past him to the stairs of the veranda.

"We can quit, you know," Brian said.

"I'll take a break. You can keep going. I think you need to work a few things out," his grandfather said, dropping onto the wooden stair and mopping his face with an oversize red hankie. "Did you truly think the factory would open again?"

Brian set his shovel aside, squatted down and

worked the clump of weeds loose from the dirt.
"It was something to hang on to while I was
working at the bakery."

"Did you love that factory job?"

Brian sat back on his haunches, frowning at
his grandfather's question. "It was a good job.
It gave me security. Paid me enough that, when
the time came, I could support a family."

"And that's important to you?"

"It is. That's why I just took a truck driving
job in Concordia. So I could take care of my
family." Not that he had any prospects for said
family anymore.

Thinking of Melissa created a sudden instant
of pain so intense he almost bent over. But he
pulled in a breath and focused on what he was
doing. He had to keep moving. Keep working.

"If you take that job, you won't be around
much," his grandfather said, thankfully still
dealing with mundane reality. "Are you sure
you want to do that?"

Brian attacked the tangle of weeds and dirt,
his mind trying to sort through the questions
his grandfather was throwing at him. "Though
I'll be on the road a lot, it's a good paying job.
A man should be able to take care of his wife.
His children. To pay the bills and give them
a roof over their head." He released a cynical

laugh. "I couldn't do that on what Melissa was paying me."

Behind all of that were the words that stung the most, though.

I don't need you.

Those four words could still create a booming hollowness in his heart.

"Did you want to support her?" Grandpa asked.

Brian jerked another weed loose. "I did, but she's too independent. That bakery is important to her and I get that. But I can't be with someone I can't be on equal footing with. It's...well..."

"Humiliating," his grandfather finished for him.

"I guess I have too much pride," Brian said. "It's who I am. I think a man should be proud to be able to take care of his family the way Dad took care of us. Mom never had to work. She could stay home."

"She chose to stay home. I think if she wanted to work your father wouldn't have cared."

"Oh, I know that," Brian said. "I'm not a chauvinist who thinks a woman has to stay home. I think it's a privilege to be able to do that for your wife." His mind ticked back to the disagreement he and Melissa had when talking about Gracie and Trent. How she thought Gracie should keep her job as a backup. Some kind of insurance against a possible breakup.

"Do you figure Melissa thinks owning the bakery is a privilege?"

"It's her dream," Brian said. "And that's okay too, but I can't be just her employee. I need to be her equal at least and until I quit, truth was she was my boss. I can't live like that. I need to bring something to the relationship and I couldn't do that working for her."

His grandfather gave him an understanding smile. "I get that." He looked back over his shoulder at the house behind him. "I love this house and I know you do, too."

Frowning, Brian tried to follow the sudden leap in the conversation, but he was willing to go along for now. "I do. It's a beautiful place."

The perfect place for a family.

"You know how I got it, don't you?"

Brian frowned. "I thought you got it from your father, Grandpa Montclair."

Grandpa laughed and shook his head. "Nope. I got it when I married your grandmother. She inherited it from her parents and when we got married, my name got put on the title. But we were partners on this property, which was rare for that time. Mostly everything was put in the man's name, but she insisted her name stay on the title. We fought about it because I thought she didn't trust me and needed a backup, but she said it was because she wanted to stay on equal footing with me." Grandpa winked at Brian. "Keep me in line so to speak. She was a feisty one. Independent, too."

Like Melissa, Brian thought.

"I knew she was feisty," Brian said with a smile, remembering arguments she and Grandpa used to have. "I just never knew that about the house."

"When your grandmother died, I sold the place to your parents and bought that house in town. Couldn't be on this place here without her. She was my better half." Grandpa's tone was careful, but Brian heard the sadness in the words.

Then Grandpa turned back to Brian. "You said you can't bring anything to your relationship with Melissa. I think maybe you need to think of what you *can* bring instead of what you can't. You own this house. I remember how dreamy-eyed she got when you came here. She loves this place."

"Well, yeah—"

"So that's the first thing," Grandpa said, raising a finger. "You can provide a home. Another thing—you were telling me some of your plans and it sounded to me like you were giving her many good ideas for her bakery."

Brian lifted his shoulder in a laconic shrug, still not convinced of what his grandfather was saying. "I did but I was still just an employee."

"Maybe you need to rethink how this could work between the two of you," his grandfather said. "You came up with good ideas for the bakery. Apply that creativity to your relationship. Is she worth fighting for?"

Brian let the words settle. Once he might have said, *Absolutely*. But now?

I don't need you.

He couldn't seem to get past those words. Brian picked up his shovel and attacked the flower bed again.

"I don't know if it's worth it because I'm not sure if she thinks I am."

"I wouldn't say that and I wouldn't make any hasty decisions. Think about this and pray about it. Let go of what you think has to happen and be open to how God wants to work in your life." Grandpa pushed his hands on his knees and stood. "I'm getting a glass of water. You want anything?"

Brian shook his head, turning over the dirt in the flower bed around a large rosebush. As he worked, he mulled over what his grandfather had told him. Maybe he had to let go of his pride. Maybe there was another way to deal with Melissa.

However, he wasn't sure what it was. He only knew his feelings for Melissa had taken root so deeply in his heart, he wouldn't be able to remove them as easily or as painlessly as the weeds he now pulled out.

And he knew that his grandfather was right. He needed to pray about this. To put everything in the hands of the One whose love was unconditional and uncomplicated.

Chapter Fourteen

"So that's it? Just like that, it's over?" Lily snapped her fingers, the sharp sound underlining the pain Melissa was dealing with. "Just before Gracie's wedding?"

Lily had come to the bakery this morning to discuss delivery of the items for Gracie's wedding. When she noticed Brian wasn't working, she started asking questions Melissa tried to avoid answering.

"I guess," Melissa said, focusing her attention on putting the final touches on the first batch of petit fours she was making for tomorrow. She'd had to work harder without Brian's help, but she couldn't sleep last night so had come here a couple of hours earlier. Amanda was doing some last-minute errands, and when she came back they would start on the buns and the rest of the pastries. The cake was already done and in the cooler, awaiting its delivery to the hall.

Now her head buzzed and her heart ached and all she wanted to do was curl up in a ball and forget everyone and everything.

You keep going and you take care of yourself.

"Will you be able to do all this by yourself?" Lily asked.

"Amanda is helping." She spoke quickly. Curtly. Struggling to suppress the quaver she felt building in her chest. She couldn't let her pain over Brian overcome her.

"I can't believe that he would walk away like that."

"He didn't walk away," Melissa said, pressing an index finger to her temple, feeling the need to defend Brian. "I drove him away. I told him I didn't need him." She looked over at Lily, as if to emphasize what she just said. "And I don't. I don't want to need someone. It hurts too much when they disappoint you. When you don't measure up to what they want."

"Is that what you think happened?"

"Brian wants a perfect wife who stays at home, and I can't be that person." She looked around the bakery, her lips lifting in a melancholy smile. "This is everything I've ever dreamed of. It's *my* dream. *My* plan. For the first time in my life I'm doing what I want and not blindly following someone else's dream." She turned back to Lily. "I'm not letting someone else's plans and dreams determine what I'm doing. I want to be in control of my life and my plans."

"Man plans and God laughs," Lily said.

"What do you mean by that?" Melissa asked, shooting her friend a puzzled frown as she boxed up the tarts she had made this morning.

Lily chuckled. "It's a way of saying we might think we're in control when everything we have and everything we are is a gift from God, given to us by grace."

"That sounds like the passage I read last night," Melissa said with a weary smile as she tucked the box flaps closed. "It was from Ephesians, something about following our own thoughts and desires, but God in His mercy gave us grace as a gift."

"Ephesians 2." Lily took the boxes from Melissa and packed them in the coolers. "I'm glad to know you're reading your Bible and seeking a relationship with God."

"I'm still struggling, but Brian has helped me there, too," Melissa said.

"How did he do that?" Lily asked, curious.

"When I told him that I didn't think God would want me back in church because I hadn't been for a while, he told me God's shoulders are broad. That He would be pleased to see me come to church and return to Him."

As Melissa spoke her heart twisted. What she and Brian had had was nothing like any relationship she'd ever had with any other man and much as she clung to her independence, a large part of her yearned for the closeness they shared on so many levels.

"You look worried," Lily said.

Melissa pressed her trembling lips together, trying not to cry. "I can't be the woman Brian wants, no matter how much I pray. But I can't stop thinking about him and I can't let go of this bakery."

"I don't think God would require that of you," Lily said. "But maybe you need to know where to put the bakery in your life."

Melissa heard the wisdom of Lily's words. She knew the bakery was all she had thought of since it had opened and the weight of making it succeed rested heavily on her shoulders.

Then Lily patted her arm. "You don't need to deal with that right now. Let's focus on this wedding. Once it's out of the way I'm sure things will be clearer."

"I don't see how," Melissa said. "But at any rate, I'll be fine."

"I'll be praying for you," Lily said, giving her a comforting pat on her shoulder before she left.

"Thanks. I'll need it," Melissa replied, then

turned her attention to the list of instructions she was compiling for Amanda.

Half an hour later the van was loaded up with items for the reception tomorrow and she was backing out of the lot behind the bakery. As she put the van in gear a shiny, candy-apple-red truck stopped at the edge of Bronson Park.

Brian's truck, she realized with a lift of her heart.

Brian stepped out, wearing blue jeans and a grimy T-shirt, his hair falling across his forehead in an appealing tangle. He pulled a couple of shovels and hoes out of the back of the truck and then he looked up.

He paused, the one shovel falling to the ground as he saw her. For a moment he just stared. Melissa's heart leaped as he took a step toward her van. But he was only bending over to pick up the shovel he dropped.

Melissa's cheeks burned, and she tore her gaze away, focusing on the road and the work ahead of her. However, as she drove to the church, she couldn't get his face out of her mind.

Chapter Fifteen

Brian smoothed his hand over his hair as he stepped into the church foyer, thinking again that he should get it cut before he started his new job. Didn't hurt to leave a good first impression.

"Good afternoon," Max, Gracie Wilson's oldest brother, said to him with a curt nod and handed him a program. "Friend of the bride or groom?"

"Bride, I guess," Brian said, taking the program and glancing over the gathering with a heavy sigh.

He hadn't counted on coming to Trent and Gracie's wedding today. The idea of attending a wedding when his own heart had been dragging around his ankles the past few days seemed too ironic.

Since his little chat with his grandfather, he'd

picked up his phone any number of times to call Melissa, but he stopped himself. She didn't want him. Didn't need him.

No man likes to hear that.

At the same time, however, he wanted to support Gracie today. He knew she had been having a few wedding jitters.

Max motioned for him to follow, and Brian had no choice but to get moving. The church was beautiful. Little clusters of flowers were attached to the end of each pew and huge bouquets filled the front.

To one side a string quartet was quietly playing music, adding an elegant ambience to the entire proceedings.

That must have cost a few dollars, Brian thought, following Max.

The church was almost full and Brian wondered where he would end up. Then Max stopped and gestured for Brian to sit down. Brian nodded, then looked over to the empty space Max had chosen for him. His heart jumped up from his heels, thundering in his chest.

Lexi Ross was moving over, smiling as she made room for him to sit down beside Melissa as if this was the most normal thing for him to do.

Of course, he thought. This was Bygones. Sitting in church together the past two Sundays had signaled to the community their intentions. Now most people assumed they were together. But there were a few glitches in the Bygones network. Obviously neither Max nor Lexi had heard about their fight.

Just then Melissa looked up from the program. The light from the stained-glass window landed directly on her auburn hair, burnishing it with multicolored light. Her soft yellow dress only served to set off the color of her hair, which she wore loose today, clipped back with a single yellow flower, and as she lifted her head, it flowed away from a suddenly pale face. Her eyes grew wide and her mouth formed a perfect O of surprise.

At least he hoped it was surprise and not anger.

More than anything he wanted to turn and leave, but people were watching and other guests were right behind him. So he straightened his shoulders and slipped into the pew between Lexi's daughter, Treena, and Melissa.

Melissa moved over to make room, but she couldn't go far because Dale Eversleigh was on the other side of her, his toupee on straight for a change.

Dale gave him a smile, added a puzzling wink, then turned away as if to give him and Melissa some privacy.

"Good afternoon, Melissa," Brian mumbled, running his finger around the collar of his shirt and feeling suddenly hot and uncomfortable in his good clothes.

"Afternoon," Melissa said, shooting a glance up at him and hurriedly glancing back at the wedding program she was clutching.

Brian cleared his throat, shifted his weight and turned and smiled at little Treena, who was staring at him. He was about to ask her about her campaign to keep the school open when she ducked her head and traded places with her brother.

Wow. He was really winning over the ladies today, Brian thought, leaning forward, resting his elbows on his knees, staring straight ahead and trying not to pay attention to Melissa sitting right beside him.

He fiddled with the program, his mind ticking over what lay ahead of him. Tomorrow he had an interview with a construction company whose owner knew Mr. Randall. They were based out of Concordia, which would mean Brian could stay in Bygones.

But it would mean he would be on the road a lot.

He shot Melissa a sidelong glance, then felt his heart turn over again.

She was looking at him, but when their eyes

met, her gaze swung away. Looking anywhere but at him, he thought.

He caught Lexi frowning at him as if trying to figure out what was going on.

He ignored her as he tried to ignore Melissa. But he was far too aware of Melissa's slender body beside his, the vague, flowery scent of her perfume, the way she crossed her feet at the ankles.

Driving a truck all over the country. Being away from home stretches at a time. He closed his eyes, trying to do what his grandfather told him. Trying to find a creative way out of the dilemma facing him. He wanted to take care of his family. To be the kind of provider someone like Melissa deserved.

Help me to trust in You, Lord, he prayed. *Help me to put You first in my life and not to get caught up in the things I want. Show me wisdom.*

It was the same prayer he had been praying ever since Melissa ordered him out of the bakery.

The string quartet kept playing and people kept filing in. After ten more torturous minutes of being too aware of Melissa beside him, thankfully the music changed.

People shifted in their pews, trying to see what was happening. Trent was escorting Mrs.

Morgan in. He brought her to her seat, then Max brought Gracie's mother into the church and returned to his spot as usher.

Trent stood at the front of the church, his hands clasped in front of him, his one foot jigging. Brian felt for the guy, but at the same time he was jealous of him. He was getting married. Going to start a family.

This was something Brian had wanted since he was a young boy. Something he thought might happen with the woman sitting beside him.

He shook those foolish thoughts off. Melissa was independent, and although he admired that, he also knew she wasn't going to give him much space in her life.

The tenor of the music changed again as Brian recognized Pachelbel's Canon flowing from the instruments. His mother had loved that piece, he thought, his heart shifting over.

He wanted to look at Melissa, feeling a need to connect with her, but he kept his gaze resolutely on the aisle. He just had to get through this wedding. Once it was over, he could leave.

The bridesmaids were coming in now on the arms of the groomsmen, their black tuxedoes a contrast to the blue silk of the bridesmaids' dresses. The girls smiled shyly, the bouquets of their flowers a bright splash of color against their dresses. He had no clue what they were, but they looked pretty.

The bridal party arranged themselves across the church, the string quartet changed their music to the classic "Bridal Chorus" and everyone stood to watch the bride and her father make their grand entrance.

The chorus went on. Still no bride and her father.

People shifted and a few murmurs rose up.

Still the quartet played and still the people waited and still no bride.

Where were Gracie and her father? Had something happened?

The quartet kept going and going. Then Max strode to the front of the church, past a frowning Mr. and Mrs. Morgan, to where the Pastor Garman stood. He bent over and whispered something in the pastor's ear.

Pastor Garman's eyes grew wide and he pressed a hand to his chest. Then he looked over the gathering and cleared his throat. "I'm afraid I have an announcement to make. The bride has apparently left the building."

The murmurs had grown to gasps of surprise.

"What? Are you kidding me?" Trent called out.

Mrs. Morgan flew to his side, taking his hand

as if to console him, but he flung it off and then stormed down the aisle, on a one-man mission to find his runaway bride.

People looked at one another, unsure of what to do.

Two of Gracie's brothers ran after him, followed by a distraught Mrs. Morgan. "Where is that girl?" she called out as if people in the audience might have an idea and were keeping it from her.

Her husband, a dapper gentleman also dressed in a tuxedo, his salt-and-pepper hair clipped short, followed Mrs. Morgan, his expression one of long-suffering.

Brian wasn't sure, but he thought he caught an expression of relief on the man's face.

Brian shifted his weight, trying to think what to do, when his arm brushed Melissa's. He started, the contact sending a jolt through him, but he forced himself to not turn to her.

He wanted to leave, to get away, and he was about to when Mrs. Morgan marched back up the aisle and up to the podium. She grabbed the microphone, her eyes glittering as she shot a glance over the gathering. "Sorry to have to say this, but I do believe we will not be having a wedding ceremony today. Thank you." Then without another word of explanation, she marched down the stairs and down the aisle, her cheeks a bright red, her head held high.

Brian heard the collective gasps of the audience reflecting his own astonishment. Now what?

People began moving and a few started down the aisle to leave. Obviously it was time to go.

Brian kept himself turned away from Melissa, but Lexi and her husband were trying to explain to their children what was going on. The only way he could get out was to turn around.

As he did, he heard a faint sniff.

Curious, he glanced Melissa's way. Her head was still lowered, her hair falling around her delicate features in thick, rich waves. Then he saw her hand come up and swipe at her cheeks. He caught a glimmer of moisture in her eyes.

Was she crying about the canceled wedding?

He watched her as she clutched the pew in front of her, her head still bent. Dale Eversleigh moved out into the aisle, but Melissa still stood there.

Brian stayed where he was.

Finally she glanced over at him and he saw her eyes rimmed with red, a smear of mascara on her cheek.

"Are you okay?" When he spoke the words, he realized how lame they sounded. Of course she wasn't okay. She was crying. Melissa had never struck him as the crying sort.

"Are you sad about the wedding? Sad for Gracie?"

"Yes, but that's not why I'm crying."

He moved closer, concern mingling with curiosity blending with his own need to connect with this woman who had occupied a huge portion of his thoughts the past few weeks.

"Tell me what's wrong."

She drew in a quivering breath, then caught his gaze. "Not here," she whispered.

"Okay. Let's go for a walk." He stilled the heavy, expectant beating of his heart. He had prayed that Melissa might hear what he had to say and here, hopefully, was his opportunity.

Don't mess up, he thought as they followed a few stragglers out of church. *Don't mess up.*

Thankfully no one waylaid either of them on their way out, and a few minutes later they were walking past the Bronson Homestead toward the park. The same place they had shared their first kiss.

A cool wind wafted across the park as they meandered their way over. When they got to the grass, Melissa bent over and took off her shoes, letting them dangle from her hand. She drew in a long breath, then eased it out as if preparing herself.

But still she said nothing. After a few minutes of silence, Brian grew uncomfortable. He didn't want to talk about the aborted wedding they had just attended, but he wasn't sure what would be a safe topic.

"So, what do you think you're going to do with all the leftover food?" He might as well start with the obvious.

"I don't know. I don't want to think about all the waste. All the work I put into everything."

"I saw you leaving Saturday for the church." And had to stop himself from jumping into the van to help her.

"It was a busy day."

"Sorry I wasn't there to help."

"You had other things on your mind. Doesn't matter now anyway, now that Gracie's wedding is off."

Brian shoved his hands in the pockets of his pants. Wow. This conversation was going well. He blew out his breath and then decided that enough was enough. He might as well do what everyone always accused him of. Go straight for the obvious.

"So why were you crying in church? You said it wasn't because of Gracie."

Melissa stopped at a picnic table in the far recesses of the park, hidden from the road by a large clump of ash trees. She ran her hands down her black skirt, then looked over at him. "No. Like I said, I felt bad for her, but I have been trying not to cry ever since you…" Her sentence faded away, the air thick with her unspoken words.

"Since I sat down beside you?" he ventured, hope growing in him.

Her only reply was a tight nod.

"Sorry about that," he murmured. "I just went where Max brought me.

"You wouldn't have sat there otherwise." She stated this as a simple fact.

"It was too hard to sit with you…beside you," he corrected.

"So both of us were in a tough spot," she said.

"I still am." The confession spilled out of him before he could stop it.

Her eyes flew to his and the emotions he saw in their shining depths gave strength to his fragile hope. Then she gave him a tremulous smile. "Things aren't the same at the bakery without you."

"I thought you didn't need me."

Melissa looked down at her hands again, weaving her fingers together. "I was wrong."

He sat down on the picnic bench behind him and, taking a chance, caught her hand and gently tugged. She took the hint and sat down beside him.

She looked over at him, her eyes still red from her tears. He pulled out a hanky and, instead of handing it to her, gently wiped an errant tear from her cheek. She sniffed, then released a shaky laugh. "I must look a fright."

"You look as amazing as always."

Melissa laughed again, then she sucked in a long, slow breath, as if preparing herself. "I don't feel so amazing."

"Why not?"

She sighed and gave him a shy look. "Like I said, I missed you."

Her admission hit him square in the chest and he caught her hands in his. "I missed you, too. So much. I wanted to come to the bakery so many times."

"Why didn't you?"

Her quiet question dove into his soul, then he released a tight laugh. "You told me you didn't need me."

Melissa sighed lightly then turned his hand over, tracing the scars across the back of them. "I was wrong."

Her words hung between them, then she looked up at him, her eyes shining with new tears.

"I do need you," she said. "In so many ways."

"Not just to bake your bread and tote around your flour bags," he said lightly.

"No. I need you beside me. I missed you."

Her admission eased the pain that had lodged in his chest ever since he walked out of the bakery. Ever since he thought they couldn't be together anymore.

Then he brushed her hair back from her damp cheeks, his fingers lingering a moment. "I need you, too. These past few days have been horrible."

"I'm glad."

He smiled at her admission, then took a chance, bent his face to hers and brushed a gentle kiss over her warm lips. She caught the back of his neck and kissed him back.

Brian felt as if his world had compressed down to this moment with Melissa. As if everything else was simply peripheral to this moment between the two of them.

"You mean more to me than anyone ever has," he whispered, tucking her head against his shoulder, thankful for this moment, thankful they were back together. For the first time since he walked away from the bakery he felt as if things were right in his world.

And for the first time in months he felt as if he was right where he was supposed to be.

"I don't want us to fight again," he said.

Melissa sighed, her breath warm against his neck. "I don't either, but I think it will happen again."

"Probably," he admitted, pulling back and fingering a strand of hair out of her face. "You're a feisty one," Brian said with a chuckle. "Just like my grandmother."

"I didn't used to be," Melissa said, her hand resting on his chest. "There was a time in my life when I...I did what I was told. No questions asked."

"What do you mean?" Brian felt as if time slowed, sensing she was about to divulge something important. "Tell me," he urged.

Melissa pulled in a breath and gave her head a light shake. "It doesn't matter."

Brian leaned back, placed a finger under her chin and tipped her face up to his. "I think it does. Tell me about you. How you got to where you are now."

Melissa looked into his eyes, as if she wasn't sure he was serious. Then he squeezed her hand to encourage her.

"I want you to know why the bakery is important to me," she said, turning away from him. She took a deep breath, her eyes taking on an inward look. "My father was a dreamer. The kind of guy who, my mom used to say, threw horseshoes at the moon. He was always planning some amazing scheme and he dragged me and my mother around until I was about five. My parents fought all the time. Finally my father left to pursue some dream about having his own fishing boat. We never heard from him again. After that my mother kind of fell apart. As a result she did the same thing to me my father did to us. We moved all over the place while she tried to figure out what she wanted, tried to figure out where she fit. The only stable place I lived during that time was with my grandmother."

"She was the one who took you to church?"

Melissa nodded, her hand clinging to Brian's as if anchoring herself.

"She introduced me to faith and I thought we had found a stable place, and then my mother finally heard from my father and we met up again. Of course, it was a disaster and off me and my mom went again. I moved out the first chance I had. I went to business school, took some baking classes on the side and then I met Jason. He chased me and pursued me and I gave in. I thought I had found someone who wanted what I wanted, but I discovered I had fallen for someone who was just like my father. Only I didn't see it right away. Jason started making plans. We were going to go into business together. I had some money and so did he. We put up a down payment on a business, a bakery, in St. Louis. We moved and then Jason took off on me. He took my money and he…" She stopped there, shaking her head. "It's so humiliating to even admit I was such a huge fool."

"Not a huge fool. Never that," Brian said, tightening his grip on hers, finally getting a glimpse of why Melissa was the way she was.

She gave him a grateful smile. "A bit of a fool then," she said with a light laugh. "Anyhow, I stayed in St. Louis and got a job working at a hotel."

"Jason was an idiot," he said. And though her relationship with Jason had been years ago he couldn't stop a sliver of jealousy. "I'm sorry he broke your heart."

Melissa released a cynical laugh. "Don't be sorry. I don't know if I was truly in love with him or just in love with the idea of being in love." She caught her lower lip between her teeth, looking down at her hands still twined in his. "I promised myself I wouldn't let any man determine the course of my life. That I would follow my own dreams—not someone else's." She heaved a heavy sigh, then looked at him, a wry smile tugging at her lips. "Then I got this chance through the SOS Committee to start up my own bakery. I didn't think I had the slightest chance, but when it came, I took it as an affirmation of what I wanted. Of part of my future."

"Only part?"

"Yeah. Part. Someday I want a family." She looked away, a flush staining her cheeks.

Her last words snagged his attention. "A family?"

Melissa nodded. "I don't know exactly when that will happen and all that, but yeah." Then she looked up at him again, her eyes holding his, an uncertain expression shifting over her face. "I want kids and a home and...well, a family. I want the kind of community and values Bygones has to offer. I want what your mom and dad had."

"So you do want kids." He knew he was repeating himself, but he had to affirm what she was saying.

"Of course I do." Her look of surprise was a surprise to him. Then her expression grew serious. "But I want my bakery, too. I think I can have both."

Brian felt as if the ground beneath him shifted. Melissa wanted a family. Now he was the one who felt like a fool. He had made wrong assumptions about Melissa. But as he gained his footing, he felt a surge of joy and relief.

"I know I can't be the kind of woman you

think I should be," Melissa said, pulling away from him. "But—"

"Stop," Brian said, touching her lips with his finger. "I don't want you to be anyone but who you are. I want you to know that your plans and dreams are important to me. I know the bakery is part of who you are and now I have a better idea of why it's important to you." He traced the curve of her eyebrow, then her lips. "I don't want you to be anyone else. I love you the way you are."

Melissa blew out a sigh that seemed to contain all the stress and concern of the past few days. "Really?" she asked, her trembling fingers threading through his unkempt hair. "You really love me?"

"Oh, yeah," Brian admitted. "These past few days have been miserable for me, but I've had time to think. I've made some of my own plans."

Melissa tilted her head, a curious glint in her eyes. "Tell me about your plans."

Brian ran his hand down her arm and caught her hands in his. "While I was working in the factory I set money aside in the hopes I could start a mechanic shop. I was turned down by the bank and when I heard about the SOS Committee I applied to them and got turned down by them, too. When my tools got stolen, I kind of figured that was the end of that dream."

"I was so sad for you when that happened," Melissa said.

"Well, you can stop being sad," Brian said. "Saturday, after me and Grandpa came back from working in the community garden, I went to put the shovels away and the tools were back, piled up in the middle of the shop."

"Why would someone steal your tools and then bring them back?"

Brian shrugged. "Not sure. I'll leave that up to Joe to solve. Whoever took them must have felt guilty. Thank goodness—because that means I don't have to replace them."

Melissa smiled up at him. "That's great," she said enthusiastically. "You can keep doing mechanic work."

"It *is* kind of great and I'll probably keep doing some on the side, but things have changed for me. I've learned how to bake bread, make flaky pie crust, bake muffins and fool around with recipes. I've discovered something I didn't think I'd ever enjoy doing."

Melissa's light frown showed him she wasn't sure where he was going.

He pressed his fingertip to the wrinkle between her eyebrows, easing it away. "I like working in the bakery and I like working with you. But I don't like being just an employee. I want to pull my own weight. To be the kind of provider you deserve. So I'm taking the money I had set aside to start my mechanic shop and, if you're willing, I want to invest it in the bakery."

Melissa's eyes grew wide with surprise. "Really?" she said, disbelief and surprise mingling in her expression. "You want to be my partner? You want to be a part of my bakery?"

"Yeah. I do."

She covered her mouth with her hand, shaking her head as if trying to absorb it.

"You're serious?"

"Yeah, and I know you won't take my money and run because you have to stick around a couple more years," he said.

"I won't do that because there's nowhere else I'd rather be and there's no one else I'd rather be with," she said, throwing her arms around his neck, hugging him so tightly he thought she would do serious damage. Then she pulled back again. "What about your job in Concordia?"

"Obviously I'm not going to have enough time for that if I'm partner in the bakery," Brian said. "Tomorrow I'm calling the company and telling them I got a better job offer."

"This is amazing."

"And I have some other ideas of how to expand the business," Brian said, her enthusiasm spilling over and creating excitement in him, too. "I've seen some bakeries selling stuff online. I think we could do the same. We'd have to figure out what kind of products we want to sell and, of course, get someone to do a website for us. I think the cake pops would be a hit as well as—"

Melissa stopped his words with a kiss.

"I get the idea," she said quietly, her eyes shining brightly. "You are an amazing guy, Brian Montclair."

"And you're an amazing woman, Melissa City Slicker Sweeney."

"City Slicker no more," she warned. "I'm a Bygones girl now."

"You're my girl now," Brian promised, holding her close to him. "And you're my partner."

"Partners," Melissa echoed. "In this together."

"Together," Bran echoed. "I'm liking the sound of that."

Then Brian sealed their promise with another kiss.

* * * * *

Dear Reader,

Brian had his own dreams and plans but he had to see them fade away while other things happened in his life—like working in a bakery, something that he never saw in his future. Yet he managed to find the positive in it, to realize that though this wasn't what he would have chosen, he ended up enjoying it. I'm sure some of you have been in situations you didn't choose, but, Lord willing, you managed to find your way through it and find the positive in it. Sometimes, blessings come in the places we least expect them.

Carolyne Aarsen

P.S. I love to hear from my readers. You can write me at caarsen@xplornet.com or check out my website at www.carolyneaarsen.com.

Questions for Discussion

1. Where do you think Melissa's need for independence came from? Did you identify with her?

2. Brian came across a bit harsh at the beginning of the book. Why do you think he reacted the way he did to Melissa and to the new shopkeepers in general? Could you sympathize?

3. How do you think Melissa felt when she found out that not all the people in town were supportive of her? How would you feel?

4. The series deals with a town going through some economic tough times. Have you had to deal with something like this? How did you cope? Did the difficulties bring you closer to your neighbors?

5. Brian was hesitant to leave Bygones. Think of some of the reasons he wanted to stay. How would you react in his situation?

6. One of the criteria for the SOS Committee giving out the money was that the per-

son receiving it must be from out of town. Why do you think the mysterious benefactor made this stipulation?

7. "I am the bread of life" was a Bible passage written on a banner in the church. How do you think this passage applied to the story?

8. Melissa and Brian were, initially, in conflict. What finally brought them together?

9. Brian felt a need to be the main breadwinner for his family. Discuss your reactions to this need. Did you feel sympathetic to his desire? Why or why not?

10. What could Brian and Melissa do at the end of the book that they couldn't do at the beginning? What did they have to change about themselves to get there?

LARGER-PRINT BOOKS!

GET 2 FREE LARGER-PRINT NOVELS PLUS 2 FREE MYSTERY GIFTS

Love Inspired®

Larger-print novels are now available...

YES! Please send me 2 FREE LARGER-PRINT Love Inspired® novels and my 2 FREE mystery gifts (gifts are worth about $10). After receiving them, if I don't wish to receive any more books, I can return the shipping statement marked "cancel." If I don't cancel, I will receive 6 brand-new novels every month and be billed just $5.24 per book in the U.S. or $5.74 per book in Canada. That's a savings of at least 23% off the cover price. It's quite a bargain! Shipping and handling is just 50¢ per book in the U.S. and 75¢ per book in Canada.* I understand that accepting the 2 free books and gifts places me under no obligation to buy anything. I can always return a shipment and cancel at any time. Even if I never buy another book, the two free books and gifts are mine to keep forever.

122/322 IDN F49Y

Name _____ (PLEASE PRINT)

Address _____ Apt. #

City _____ State/Prov. _____ Zip/Postal Code

Signature (if under 18, a parent or guardian must sign)

Mail to the Harlequin® Reader Service:
IN U.S.A.: P.O. Box 1867, Buffalo, NY 14240-1867
IN CANADA: P.O. Box 609, Fort Erie, Ontario L2A 5X3

Are you a current subscriber to Love Inspired books and want to receive the larger-print edition?
Call 1-800-873-8635 or visit www.ReaderService.com.

* Terms and prices subject to change without notice. Prices do not include applicable taxes. Sales tax applicable in N.Y. Canadian residents will be charged applicable taxes. Offer not valid in Quebec. This offer is limited to one order per household. Not valid for current subscribers to Love Inspired Larger-Print books. All orders subject to credit approval. Credit or debit balances in a customer's account(s) may be offset by any other outstanding balance owed by or to the customer. Please allow 4 to 6 weeks for delivery. Offer available while quantities last.

Your Privacy—The Harlequin® Reader Service is committed to protecting your privacy. Our Privacy Policy is available online at www.ReaderService.com or upon request from the Harlequin Reader Service.

We make a portion of our mailing list available to reputable third parties that offer products we believe may interest you. If you prefer that we not exchange your name with third parties, or if you wish to clarify or modify your communication preferences, please visit us at www.ReaderService.com/consumerchoice or write to us at Harlequin Reader Service Preference Service, P.O. Box 9062, Buffalo, NY 14269. Include your complete name and address.

LILPDIR13R

REQUEST YOUR FREE BOOKS!
2 FREE WHOLESOME ROMANCE NOVELS
IN LARGER PRINT
PLUS 2
FREE
MYSTERY GIFTS

❈❈❈❈❈❈❈❈❈❈❈❈❈❈❈❈❈❈❈❈❈❈

HEARTWARMING™

❈❈❈❈❈❈❈❈❈❈❈❈❈❈❈❈❈❈❈❈❈❈

Wholesome, tender romances

YES! Please send me 2 FREE Harlequin® Heartwarming Larger-Print novels and my 2 FREE mystery gifts (gifts worth about $10). After receiving them, if I don't wish to receive any more books, I can return the shipping statement marked "cancel." If I don't cancel, I will receive 4 brand-new larger-print novels every month and be billed just $4.99 per book in the U.S. or $5.74 per book in Canada. That's a savings of at least 23% off the cover price. It's quite a bargain! Shipping and handling is just 50¢ per book in the U.S. and 75¢ per book in Canada.* I understand that accepting the 2 free books and gifts places me under no obligation to buy anything. I can always return a shipment and cancel at any time. Even if I never buy another book, the two free books and gifts are mine to keep forever.

161/361 IDN F47N

Name _____ (PLEASE PRINT) _____

Address _____ Apt. # _____

City _____ State/Prov. _____ Zip/Postal Code _____

Signature (if under 18, a parent or guardian must sign) _____

Mail to the **Harlequin® Reader Service:**
IN U.S.A.: P.O. Box 1867, Buffalo, NY 14240-1867
IN CANADA: P.O. Box 609, Fort Erie, Ontario L2A 5X3

* Terms and prices subject to change without notice. Prices do not include applicable taxes. Sales tax applicable in N.Y. Canadian residents will be charged applicable taxes. Offer not valid in Quebec. This offer is limited to one order per household. Not valid for current subscribers to Harlequin Heartwarming larger-print books. All orders subject to credit approval. Credit or debit balances in a customer's account(s) may be offset by any other outstanding balance owed by or to the customer. Please allow 4 to 6 weeks for delivery. Offer available while quantities last.

Your Privacy—The Harlequin® Reader Service is committed to protecting your privacy. Our Privacy Policy is available online at www.ReaderService.com or upon request from the Harlequin Reader Service.

We make a portion of our mailing list available to reputable third parties that offer products we believe may interest you. If you prefer that we not exchange your name with third parties, or if you wish to clarify or modify your communication preferences, please visit us at www.ReaderService.com/consumerschoice or write to us at Harlequin Reader Service Preference Service, P.O. Box 9062, Buffalo, NY 14269. Include your complete name and address.

HWDIR13R